PROJECT
ODDITY

PROJECT
ODDITY:

The Psychological Tragedy

EKERE ANNO

iUniverse, Inc.
New York   Bloomington

Project Oddity
The Psychological Tragedy

iUniverse books may be ordered through booksellers or by contacting:

iUniverse
1663 Liberty Drive
Bloomington, IN 47403
www.iuniverse.com
1-800-Authors (1-800-288-4677)

ISBN: 978-1-4502-2378-2 (sc)
ISBN: 978-1-4502-2379-9 (ebk)

Printed in the United States of America

iUniverse rev. date: 08/26/2010

PROLOUGE

It began in the year 2012; in this year the earth was struck by waves of giant asteroids which brought: the melting of glaciers, dramatic climate change, volcanic eruptions, and great cities fell beneath the cold and pitiless waves. The ground opened up and swallowed whatever remained; good men and innocent children were engulfed so dispassionately-- just as the Mayan calendar predicted so long ago. The asteroid also spread an unknown virus throughout the planet. This airborne plague destroyed everything it touched, including the livestock & harvest. One third of the human population was killed in less than a year. But however, the courses of this cosmic calamity were studied under close scientific provisions. This is the oldest and most ancient of truth; the circle of life expands deep into the cosmos. We can come to this accord; all life was created by a great impact. The book of Noah, the great flood, was a result of a great impact. A great impact destroyed the dinosaurs so long ago and made room for us humans to dwell. Our homes were built on top of the bones of those who could not escape their fates. The circle of life will repeat itself, how will we escape our fates this time?

Dr. Eugene Osco proposed that the remaining humans; which were not infected, be placed into a spaceship code named, "The Iron Bison". The uninfected survivors quickly entered this Noah's Arch in hopes of escaping the cruel vacuole of the fatal impact. They discourteously abandoned their friends, family and lovers, and did what humans do best… survive. For that reason the dying citizens gave it the street name, "Loveless".

The loveless fled.

…And the Earth was no more.

After six years of fruitless search they find another planet they can call home. They named this planet Nirvana with hopes that it would be a world free from pain and suffering and hatred; and all those devastating emotions that had plagued their former world. This planet was shaded with the color blue and carried two beautiful moons within its orbit. But little did the humans know that within this wonderfully painted world carried an evil secret.

"This planet is the cold aftermath of a great war", the humans pleaded. "We ran away from home! I thought we escaped the darkness. This land… it cries to me. The married bones of kings and queens—the weeping souls of children and wise sages all say the same thing in such a bone chilling whisper. We should never have come here".

Some time went by as the humans worked like ants to create a colony they proudly named Mute City; in regards to the dead silence they had stumbled upon. Soon after the city's creation came a man named Felix Crown. He had white hair, haunting yellow eyes, and was of average length; but what was most distinguishing about this man was the two unusual gloves he wore on his left and right arms. The gloves had holes from the knuckles to the elbow. Felix demanded that all humans worship him like a god. The humans quickly refused and as punishment for their defiance, he destroyed much of the city they had worked so hard to build.

"Unbelievable! He did that with his own two hands? How can one man have so much power? Maybe he really is a god." Dr. Eugene Osco was the only man who rejected the thought of Felix Crown being a god. He knew that if Felix was as strong as he seemed then it must have been due to those unusual gloves he wore. Osco was obsessed with the gloves, obsessed with Felix Crown's power. He wanted to know everything there was to know about those gloves. The best scientists are the most curious and the ones that take the most risks.

After much study, he came to the conclusion that only people that were native to the planet could use the glove's power, the holes in the gloves are where the stones are kept. The stones allow the user to control any element. For example the fire stone gives the user the ability to control and create fire. While a wind stone would allow the user to control and create wind. <u>But once a native puts on the glove it could not be removed.</u>

Felix appeared in Mute City once again but this time he stole the Iron bison. It was clear that Felix was a threat to humanity. Dr. Osco then dedicated the rest of his life to creating a group of super soldiers that would utilize the same substance which could bring forth man kind's destruction. It was a giant risk. He called these soldiers the oddity. There were twelve members in this group. Each were genetically altered humans. Emotionless dolls designed to carry out tasks without a conscious. All twelve members of the oddity wore gloves much like Felix Crown.

The citizens hated the Oddity. They saw them as a weapon with a mind. They felt man could not be trusted with that much power and power would only lead to corruption. It was at that moment that they devised an evil plan. They would allow the soldiers to do battle with Felix and when they returned weak from battle, they would kill the soldiers. But something strange happened, not only was the leader of the Oddity (leader-one) killed but the remaining eleven members requested that they all resign from the military and start a real life. Dr. Osco granted them this final wish, seeing that they were not emotionless as he had hoped.

Chapter One

The Bitter End

"Somebody help me! Somebody please help me! For god's sake somebody... anybody... help me. Don't let me die here! Don't let me die alone. Please help me; Mother, grandpa, Zeke, Nyru, Johnny, Vince, Kyle, Shadow, Elliot, Jin, Donté, Father ... anybody?! Help me. Please help me. Don't say no to me—you shouldn't say no to me."

The candle of my life burns dimly. All my efforts have been exhausted. I still couldn't believe this was happening. If there is a guardian angel watching... then, where is he? Come save me.

Once again I am alone in the darkness. Trapped in a location that is unfamiliar to me. Shouting for help and ignored by those that can hear me. But I suppose I deserved this punishment. It is human nature to defy the will of god and create a monster, just as it is a monster's instinct to destroy its creator. I, Chase Vega, have done terrible things— unforgivable things to good people. I've killed dozens of people because I was blinded by a zealous desire. Who can ever love this monster that I've become?

I just wanted to see the parents that abandoned me once more, even if it meant walking through the myths of hell and leaving a path of corpses behind. Without my mother I was all alone. I hated the feeling of loneliness. That feeling was once a mystery to me, that is, before that day. Now as I look around, there is no one near or far, I am alone. I will die alone too.

I rattled the chains that restrained me in frustration. The rattles of the metal chain echoed and expanded to the outside perimeters of the jail cell. The noise was received in the ears of two eager guards, who then came to the realization that it was indeed time to rid themselves of the child that had caused everyone so much pain.

"What's that noise", I questioned. Afterwards I realized that it was the steps of the guards coming closer and closer.

"Is it time already?"

The lights in the jail cell flickered and revealed my best friend. "Kyle", I said in disbelief. "Is that you under all that red paint?"

His body was chained to the wall much like my own. The chains were strapped so tight that it allowed little room to breathe. Kyle's body was drenched in blood. His rags were too beaten and torn up to be called clothing. He lifted his head up slowly until his eyes met my own. His eyes were filled with so much hate.

"Hate for me", I wondered.

I wanted to apologize for what I've done; and all that's happened… but I couldn't find the courage to speak. I could see that he was in a great deal of pain because his head shivered violently.

Kyle's head collapsed and he now began to look at the drips of blood which flowed beneath his feet. He wore a plastic smile, telling me that things would be alright.

"Kyle", I said uneasily. "I'm sorry; this whole thing is my fault."

The guards opened the door to our prison then freed me from my shackles. While the other dragged me out of the prison. The second guard remained in the prison with Kyle. I looked back in the jail cell, wanting to know what would become of my best friend. Kyle gave me his final pretentious smile, then, the second guard delivered brutal jabs to the face of the once mighty Kyle Bison, while Kyle was powerless in defending himself. It became increasingly difficult to bear.

"No", I shouted in a burst of rage. "Kyle is not the one who should get beaten, it should be me! I caused all of this, I am deceptive, manipulative, a coward, selfish, and weak... I should be beaten, not him. I lack courage; I should be punished!"

My heart burned with undying rage. I used whatever bit of energy I had left to push away from the guard's grip, but it failed. I now had no choice but to walk away as my best friend endured every devastating blow, which resembled pounding drums.

The guard dragged my body to the foot of the clock tower, and tossed me to the ground like trash. This tower was the only standing structure in Mute City, and I was to blame for this. Below the tower was a sea of people, a sea of survivors who gathered themselves with a common purpose. To witness the death of the boy who was destined to bring forth man kinds fatal destruction.

"Mother", I cried. "My life will end in five or six minutes. Why haven't you come to save me? Am I undeserving of your love? Have you abandoned me once more, or perhaps you have also been waiting for the bitter end?

"Mother", I whispered softly to myself. "If you are indeed amongst the spectators who wished for my death, if you are near me, then will you grant me this final favor? Please sing to me once more the song of emotions, as only you can. Sing to me that song which fills my heart with joy and happiness. Sing it to me as I lay on my concrete death bead. Sing it to me till the vultures pick out all the flesh from my bones.

One of the guards dragged a short legged table to the center of the stage. What was strange to me was that the top of the table was painted dark red. He placed that horrible table right there—right in front of me. I saw another guard from the corner of my eyes drawing nearer and nearer. I slowly turned my head to satisfy my sense of wonder and curiosity. The man was dressed in an all black robe but what was most peculiar was that he held a giant sharp edged axe, it had blood all over.

"Spread your hands across the table", said the man. I looked at the bloody table and immediately understood why it was this way. They were killing all my friends; they were killing members of the once honorable Oddity.

I took another glance at the red colored table and could see the shards of bones, flesh and tiny chunks of human body parts left by other Oddity members. These were the remains of my allies, the remains of my good friends. I could almost hear their sweet voices calling out to me. I didn't cry; I was furious! I didn't know my heart was capable of such hatred until this moment. Why, if I only had a bit more time— if someone could just stall the grim reaper for ten or fifteen more minutes then I'm sure the power would return to me. Then I would be unstoppable once again. Then I'll rescue Kyle and show these bastards who was boss!

"Put your arm on the table", the man repeated impatiently.

"You can't do this to me", I shouted.

"My name is Chase India Vega from the mighty Zodant tribe! I am the son of the hero Reece Vega; I've been your eternal protector, your allies and you're kind friend. Have you all grown blind and deaf to your hero's cries? How dare you treat me this way! Are you even scarcely aware of the decisions that I had to make? I could have destroyed all of you and with it, all that you faugh so damn hard to create. I am a hero. I AM A HERO!"

The entire country viewed me as an enemy; the same country that I spent my entire life trying to protect now viewed me as an enemy.

I questioned their belief in God and they replied to me saying that it was their unassailable belief in God that validates this course of action. They whipped me like an animal until all my strength for resistance fled. They unfolded my belligerent hands and pinned it tightly on the repulsive hard wood table. I cried like the helpless child that I was and begged again for someone to come and save me. Everyone I knew was gone… and soon I lost the will to live. Soon I would be gone too.

"Nobody is coming", I whispered to myself.

"Please don't cut off my hands."

The man lifted his bloody axe.

I had nowhere else to turn to, so I prayed to God like all desperate men do. I wished that the stories I've read were true because in the end we would all have to answer to God. I dreamed and hoped and smiled from the fact that God's punishment was waiting for these men, and that it would greatly outweigh any excruciating punishment felt here on earth. That gave me something worth dying for. I shut my eyes so tight that not one single tear could escape. I could sense that the blade had reached the top and was descending with its lethal and maximum velocity.

I could hear the savage beating of the drums still and then there was another sound. This sound was tranquil, blissful and melancholy. It moved to the rhythm of a broken heart. This second sound moved synchronized with the beating drums. This second sound put my mind and spirit at ease. This second sound was unmistakably the song of emotions. I looked into the crowd with a smile on my face, keeping calm in the hour of my fatal destruction. She was there in the crowd, singing; she wore that slippery dress that I liked so much. "Thank you mother", I whispered to myself. Death is what all living creatures fear deep inside.

I bid a final farewell to my mortal body.

The axe slammed into the hard table. I was overwhelmed with pain and shouted till my throat grew horse. I shouted until the very muscles in my mouth ripped apart! The black lump in my throat was too big to swallow. The pain I felt was beyond what any man should ever be forced to endure.

The guard lifted my detached arms from the bloody table and held it proudly to the people in the crowd as if it were the most tantalizing trophy. The pain from it all had pinned me into submission. I fell to the ground hearing nothing but the cheers and applause from the people in the crowd. I reached the final stage of death, acceptance.

Chapter Two

Synthetic Life

"Reece wake up!" wake up Reece! For god's sake Reece get up there getting closer. C'mon I've gone too far; I know you're still alive. Let me hear your voice…let me hear your voice.

A small woman dragged me out of a tank filled with thick liquid, the liquid covered my body and my clothes were absent. The woman had several gray hairs and looked like she was in her late 40's. Dirt filled her clothing, while darkness covered the air. This room was strange to me. There were thousands of tanks much like my own. Each filled with that same thick liquid and contained a man inside. Each tank had its own light bulb, which chipped away the darkness, allowing the viewer to see both the face of the man within the tank and their name plate. There was a tank directly in front of me, which caught my eye. This tank was the same size as the others and possessed an equal amount of light. But what was different about this tank was the fact that there was a child inside it. The name Kyle Bison was written on the name plate. I turned around in curiosity and on my tank read the name Reece Vega.

"Reece", began the small woman with tears on her face "you don't remember me do you? You don't know what's been happening lately. You don't know any more or less than what's written on that name plate. Follow me Reece, and I will answer all your questions."

I had nowhere else to turn to, so I did just as she said. I never let my guard down; I followed this woman with such immeasurable caution. She led me to a small and vacant room, and then revealed clothing that she had safely stashed away. It was clear now that she had planned my rescue from the very beginning. She handed me the clothes with both hands. As I was putting the clothes on I noticed a puddle of water which I used as a mirror. My hair was light brown and flowed to my shoulder line. I had a fuzzy chin and a very muscular body type. I liked to be in my mid twenties and felt no taller than five foot ten inches. The clothes she gave me were mediocre. The pants fit casually, the boots were worn down and she also gave me a dark leather coat—which I found to be the most pleasing. When I finished changing she wrapped a black bandana around my head to hide my messy hair in the same manner in which a lover would. I was an overall handsome man. But there was still so much I did not understand—so many things I was unaware of.

"You said that you would answer all my questions", I said to the small woman. "Where are we? Who are you? Why am I here?

"I am Clair Vega", the small woman responded. I am your mother and only guardian. "My mother", I interrupted. "But why are we here and why are you in such a poor condition?

"I'm afraid you are to blame for this", she said in dismay. "You see, the first Reece Vega was a descendent of the original Oddity. He believed that since he possessed that bloodline that he was superior. It was that pre-conceived judgment that led him to a path of self righteous arrogance. Reece now wears those gloves and stands tall as Felix Crown's most capable advocate. Reece Vega is a cruel man, anxiety, hatred, and determination shape and form the content of his heart and mind. Felix Crown, through Reece's countless success, thought it would be wise to clone this loyal soldier. The second Reece would have equal strengths and the ability to transform into a beast. You are the second Reece; I freed you from that tank because I couldn't allow you to be another one of Felix's advocates. Right now we are inside the iron Bison. I am a prisoner in this ship, while you, my son, are merely a copy of the original."

"A copy of an original", I thought to myself.

The alarm went off, they knew I had escaped, but she continued her speech. "This is a sign from God; sometimes he'll take you through hell just to get to heaven. We can begin a new and better life, new memories. Our need serves to be our justification."

My mother broke off a pipe from one of the machines that were in the room and ran through a narrow path. She hit anyone who dared cross her way until we came to a storage room. There were three people waiting for us in that room. One of them sat on a chair while the other two stood. The one sitting had pail ghost like skin, white hair, and haunting yellow eyes. The other looked like a reflection of me. The last guy was about seven feet tall. He was bald and had large muscular arms. A huge elevator caught my mother's eyes, but before we could get to it Felix ordered Panic to attack. The bald headed, muscle bound giant then came charging towards us. I pulled my mother securely behind me, and prepared to fight this demon.

With one hit to the chest I was out cold and on the floor gasping for air. My chest felt like it would explode. He kicked me several times while I was on the ground. He soon grew bored of this and then switched to punching. My mother came to my rescue and swung the pipe at the back of his head. The pipe snapped into two and Panic turned around enraged. He quickly forgot about me and now focused on my mother. Panic grabbed her by the neck and threw her across the room like a rag doll. This made me very upset. At that same time I felt like something living inside of me wanted to get out. I could feel my body changing. I slowly began to lose control but I tried hard to fight it.

Felix snapped his fingers and Panic stopped his attack. My body regained its normal form. I slowly walked to where my mother's body lay. She could barely stand so I offered her a shoulder as we walked towards the elevator. "Don't worry mother. I said soothingly. "Everything is gonna be alright,"

I began to question why Felix let us go. Perhaps it was because I was too weak to aid him and too weak to be considered a threat. Before we could reach the elevator I heard Felix say "never show your back to the enemy." A gunshot came soon after. The bullet hit my mother on the back. Some of her blood found its way on me. She fell to the ground hard, and agony tore her eyes wide open. The feeling I had earlier came back, something inside of me wanted to come out. I could feel my whole body changing. I began to lose control again but this time I didn't fight it. My heart began to race, my eyes turned red, my hands turned into claws, black hairs grew all over my body. The wolf in me was finally unleashed and Panic was my first victim.

Chapter Three

Revenge

I slammed his body into the wall. And then I slashed him repeatedly with my claws. He threw me to the ground but I got back up just as quickly. Panic now carried a scar on his chest which ran from his left shoulder to his right waist. He slowly fell to the ground. His right hand wrapped around his chest in a feudal attempt to suppress the pain. I ran towards him, wanting to make most of his suffering. Then I punched him again, and again, until I saw that color that linked itself to death. Panic got up in a burst of rage and punched me to the familiar ground. I coughed out a tremendous amount of blood. Standing on two feet was a nearly impossible mission. That punch felt like being shot by a cannon ball. Panic approached me slowly, grabbed me by the neck and lifted me up. I swung at him, but he grabbed my hand and snapped my wrists back. I screamed helplessly in tremendous agony as he continued to crush my wrist. He then bashed his head into my own then threw my body to the ground. My body changed back to human form and it became so very clear that I could not win.

The elevator was directly behind me. If I wished to continue life on this world then I had to get out of this ship. I grabbed my mother's lifeless body and ran as fast as I could inside the elevator.

A cowardly move I suppose, but cowards tend to live longer.

Inside the elevator was quiet. All that could be heard was the grinding and churning sound of the rising elevator along with my heavy beating heart. The elevator came to an abrupt stop. I stepped out of the elevator with such inexplicable caution. The elevator traveled back down to the storage room. It was cold on top of the Iron Bison. The heavy rain pounded on my bruises, making life more difficult. The ship stood thousands of feet in the air. I searched for a way down and was grateful to find a supply department with an air craft inside. I limped slowly towards the air craft, leaving behind a trail of my mother's blood. I firmly strapped my mother on the passenger's seat. As I climbed into the driver's seat, I heard the sound of the elevator coming back up. My whole body began to shake. I knew that it was Panic and he had returned to finish the job. I smashed my fingers all over the air craft trying to figure out a way to get it started. By the time I had gotten it started Panic had punched his hand through the glass and dragged me out of the air craft. Sharp pieces of glass were now lunged into my body. I was bleeding all over. I grabbed a chain that was tied to the roof of the supply department and climbed up it. I planned to stay up here as long as possible. Panic jumped and grabbed onto my feet. I lost grip of the chain and was now at his mercy. He held me upside down, but before he could strike me, I tied the chain around his arm. He yanked the chain and the roof of the supply department collapsed and buried him. I used this time wisely and crawled into the air craft. After I flew away I looked back and saw that Panic had gotten out of the rubble.

It was dark inside the air craft. The night was lit by only the moons; an insufficient amount of light made me a blind navigator. I didn't know how to slow it down but I did know how to steer. The air craft descended until I approached the forest. I still didn't know how to slow it down. The next thing I knew I was traveling over one hundred miles an hour swerving through an endless amount of trees. One of the trees hit the air craft and sent it plunging into the ground with my mother and myself inside it.

I regained consciousness after some time and noticed that the air craft was on fire. I quickly abandoned all knowledge of my physical wounds and began to run towards the aircraft. The engine exploded and the impact lunged me back words. I suffered minor burns. I could hear the sound of someone growing nearer, the midnight flare must have signaled my location to my enemy. But my fears were overwhelmed by exertion and desperation.

Chapter Four

Harm of Will

I woke up the next morning from shifting dreams of darkness. I was in a wooden room. To my surprise, all my wounds were wrapped and cared for. I jolted up from my bed and searched around the room for my mother, but I had already known the answer. She was gone. I tried so hard to protect her; I gave my sweat, blood and tears to keep her by my side just a little bit longer. Was I selfish in doing so?

I found a form of love... with dragging steps, I near myself more and more to the dwindling gates of my mortality. Flowers grow towards the sun, a war lord marries Peace, wolves sing romantic songs to the moon, and the loveless die searching for love. This is the fate of all living creatures; to seek out that which we are destined to be without. It is a harm of will, the thread of our salvation.

This is that in which I posses... my mind. The heart, like many delicate organs, can be replaced but the mind cannot. So I hold these thoughts with greater value.

What am I? I'm not one of God's creations; neither a beast nor a man. Am I just some creature pretending to be human? I posses a pretentious body and a synthetic soul; I'm a vessel without a cause. My past is unknown. Can a man without a past have a future? Am I just a clone of the original Reece Vega? Why exactly do I exist? What is my purpose in life; perhaps my purpose is to be the only man without a purpose?" My mind was subdued by loneliness and began to drift into the unknown.

A beautiful woman walked in the room. Her skin was like milk chocolate. Her eyes were green like the living earth, and her hair was as dark as night. She walked in with a tray filled with food and set it on the table near my bed. She looked into my eyes and with a smile said "I'm glad you're feeling better."

I was smiling.

"Were you the one who rescued me", I asked.

"Yes", she replied. "My name is Rosaria. My father Seven and I saw the smoke from the burning air craft and rushed to your rescue. You are very lucky to be alive."

She brought out the spoons and forks and started to feed me; knowing that my beaten up body put a strict limit to my movement. We spoke to each other for a great deal of time. She explained to me that I had been lying motionless on the bed for about a week. It was implied that she had been taking care of me every day.

She picked up the dirty dishes and walked through the door, after the food was done and my stomach was satisfied. The descending sun allowed the planets two moons to shine brightly. Seven and Rosaria were probably both fast asleep.

I decided to use this time to leave; to run far away from this place. I cared about Rosaria and couldn't bear to see anything bad happen to her, should Panic come looking for me. I felt that destruction came with love, and the best way to keep the ones I cared for safe was to distant myself from them.

As I opened the front door I could see an old brown faced man waiting for me. He had long gray hair, was of equal height and had black eyes. This was the father that Rosaria had mentioned earlier; this was Seven.

"Where are you gunna run away to", he questioned.

I was unable to answer his question. There was no place I could go;

no place could I call home. I'm well now and back to my feet, I shouldn't over stay my welcome.

"I examined your wounds", he began. "That air craft we found you in was from the Iron Bison. You escaped from Felix and his followers. You fear that they will hunt you down and put everyone dear to you in danger. Running away is no course of action. We risked our lives to save you; our blood will be on your hands, if we should be slayed. Reece, your greatest fear is to live and die without a purpose. I believe that everything happens for a reason. It was no accident that we rescued you. Rosaria told me that you lost your memory. Maybe you lost it because your memory was of bad content, or maybe you're destined for a different path."

I sat down and listened to every word he had to say. I hoped that Seven would be the one who would put value to my life. I wished that he would give a purpose to this image who tries to be human.

"I am the seventh member of the Oddity", he began. We thought we killed Felix so many years ago, but he has returned, unaffected by the hands of time. I, on the other hand, have grown old and brittle. However, every member kept the gloves, which served as the source of their power. A secret army is forming called the new Oddity. I want you to inherit my glove. You can help stop Felix Crown and protect incent lives. You'll be given the power to make sure that no-one ever has to go thru what you felt."

I accepted his offer and trained to be an Oddity soldier. Maybe it was destiny that we found each other. And deep down I truly wanted to see Rosaria once more.

Chapter Five

Revealing a Bitter End

"If it is a girl then I will name her Luna," I began. "And if it is a boy then I will name him Chase. I pray that I receive a girl, so I can raise her to be like my mother, who I loved so dearly."

Many months have gone by and Rosaria Vega has given birth to our son Chase India Vega. Seven carried the child from his mother's arms to say, "welcome to existence young Chase Vega, and may your presence bring joy and happiness to those who are fortunate enough to be in your company."

"So explain to me again why we're doing this", I asked Rosaria in confusion.

"I am part of a native tribe called the Zoedants," my wife replied. "But Felix Crown has brought the extinction of most of my people. Only three people remain, myself, the oracle who lives in these forests, and Chase Vega who is half Zoedant. It is traditional to bring a new born Zoedant to an Oracle so the world may be aware of the great things to come from the child."

"A psychic", I said unwillingly. "You know I don't believe in all this psychic crap, but if it's culture then I won't be one to disapprove."

My wife turned her neck and smiled at me. She hugged chase tightly with both hands, while Chase's head rested firmly on his mother's shoulder. Seven also came along. I too wanted to know what would become of my only son. It seemed that curiosity was dominant.

Rosaria led us deeper and deeper into the forest. I grew more impatient with every step. She then stopped walking; Seven and I did the same. She pointed to a hut made of clay and said, "This is where the Oracle sleeps."

She approached the Oracle's home confidently. The hut had curtains instead of doors, so my wife banged at the walls of the hut.

"Who goes there", demanded the Oracle.

"It is I, Rosaria Vega, Rosaria of the sea shore. I bring to you my child. I wish to learn his destiny."

"Come on in", replied the Oracle. "Please excuse the un-cleanliness; I'm not use to having visitors."

Rosaria and Seven lifted the curtains and walked in. I was the last to enter. I was still not comfortable with the idea of being able to read the future. In a sense, I was afraid of what the future would hold. And I might double her honesty.

Inside the hut was petit, providing little room to move about. The ground was muddy from a previous rain. Her bed was made of leaves and wood. We all found a piece of wood to site on. The Oracle was very old and ugly. I had never seen anything so horrible looking in my life. Her sagging flesh was covered with wrinkles, huge bags lay under her fading green eyes, little gray hairs grew from her scalp sporadically, and blemishes covered her face; each filled with puce.

She reached out her wrinkled hands as Rosaria gave her our child. She then began to play with Chase. She pinched his cheeks and made childish noises. What was surprising to me was that Chase, in return, laugh, giggled and clapped playfully; when I had expected him to cry and to fear this creature's presence. This whole thing made me sick.

The Oracle then turned her neck and said, "Do you have lemons in your mouth Reece Vega, or is my presence unbearable."

"How did she know my name", I thought to myself. "Can she really be a psychic? No, don't be ridiculous. Rosaria probably told her my name." The Oracle placed both of her hands on Chase's skull, then closed her eyes. The room grew quiet. Seven and Rosaria observed carefully in silence. Even Chase was silent. I grew more impatient.

The Oracle's hands shivered violently then she pulled it away from Chase's skull as if she was shocked by electricity. The playful look she had earlier quickly turned to fear. "What had she seen in my son's future that could have caused such a drastic change", I wondered

"Rosaria of the sea shore", said the Oracle, tell me the truth. "Why have you brought me this child?"

"We live in a world of uncertainty", she answered. We live in a time that the strong rule and the week are replaceable. With the Zoedant and the Oddity being hunted down, my child, who is Zodant and Oddity may not live to see tomorrow. But as his mother I feel I must know and that's why I came to you. Please Oracle; I must know what will become of my child!"

"Do you want to know the truth about this child's future", asked the Oracle. "But I must warn you… you will be unhappy with the truth."

The Oracle looked at the faces of everyone in the room, making sure we were all paying attention. It was obvious she did not want to repeat whatever horrible news she had discovered.

"You, Reece Vega", said the Oricle. "You will raise your son to the best of your abilities. You will provide everything he needs, food, water, love, nurture… and when he grows big and strong, when he becomes the most powerful of the Oddity… that's when he'll kill you.

We were left in a quandary. "Should we raise young Chase Vega and allow him to grow into the killer he was destined to be", I thought to myself. "Or should we abandon this child and let him be someone else's burden."

"No", I said casting away the thought. As we walked back home Rosaria claimed that, "a mother should never abandon her child." And Seven refused the idea simply because he needed a grandson.

We laughed our way home. But the Oricle's words haunted me. So when the night was dark I armed myself and raced deep into the forest.

"That deceptive witch must die", I said to myself.

I finally came across the clay building where the Oracle lived. It was very dark in the forest, but the two moons provided a sufficient amount of light. I intruded into her home and was shocked to see that she was in the same position since we last met. She didn't seem to be threatened by my presence at this hour.

"You're late Reece Vega", said the Oracle with a blank expression. "Perhaps you lost your way around the forest. Or maybe you waited a bit longer to guarantee that everyone was asleep." She looked at my pocket to see the knife I had carried with me. "I don't even know why you bothered to bring that", she began. We both know that you'd rather put those powerful gloves to the test and kill me with your own two hands."

I dropped the knife to the ground. "If you knew I would come then why would you not flee", I questioned.

"It's simple my friend", replied the Oricle. One's destiny cannot be changed nor altered. The future cannot be changed. History is already written in stone. We oracles have a great understanding of that. Life is so difficult and complicated. Since death is the opposite of life, then death must be easy and simple. What are you waiting for? Serve your purpose; it's what you traveled all this way to do."

I grabbed her by the neck and lifted her tiny body into the air. With her last breath she said, "I pray for the day your son will kill you." I slammed her body into the clay wall in a burst of rage. The impact was so intense that it cracked the clay wall. I held her lifeless body in the air for a long time. Until all my hate was no more.

"Thump", she hit the ground.

I spent a great deal of time thinking of where to hide her body. But then I realized how lonesome this woman really was.

"You will rote away in this empty hut all alone", I said smiling at my success. "Nothing but the worms and maggots will come looking for you." I coughed up something so defile, and then I spat it on her face. "Amazing", I thought to myself. "These gloves give me a tremendous amount of power. Killing the Oracle was like snapping a toothpick in two... and I barely scratched the surface of its true power. Just imagine what I could be capable of with more practice. I kicked the Oracles lifeless body into the shadows where her hideous face could not be seen. I then headed home with satisfaction and a goal to become the strongest.

As I reached my home I noticed a dark figure standing in front of my house. It was almost as if this person was waiting for me. But I was more eager than afraid. I secretly hoped that this person would give me a reason to test out more of my powers. I approached the figure confidently.

"Rosaria", I said with surprise. "What are you still doing up?"

"You killed the Oricle didn't you", she began. "The Oracle is dead isn't she?"

I couldn't find the courage to speak... so I just didn't say anything. But she found the answer in my solitude.

"When I was young my mother took me to that same Oracle. The Oracle told me I would fall in love with a man who knows not of his own past. That man would be strong as well as vengeful. She told me that I would marry that man and when two hearts become one, a child would be born. She told me she would die days after the child's birth, by the hands of the child's father. You are that man Reece. Don't you understand? The Oracle is never wrong. History cannot be changed."

Chapter Six

Oracle's Gift

I once thought that it was impossible to obtain happiness during the time of my mother's death. But now I realize that I was mistaken. My wooden home over looks a beautiful waterfall and every morning I am awakened by the singing of birds. Rosaria, Seven, and Chase are always with me. I've come a long way from not having anyone. Loneliness has now become a mystery.

Today was April 24th, my son's fifth birthday. Most fathers would be happy to see their child grow up, but I was terrified. The Oracle told me five years ago that when my son grows big and strong he would kill me. I fear this day. This boy, chase, gets stronger with every breath he takes. One can only imagine his true potential. He is indeed a handsome boy; he has his mother's black hair and my skin complexion. What stands out most about this child was his gray eyes; powerful innocent, and vulnerable gray eyes.

Rosaria and Seven have both given their gifts to Chase. I, on the other hand, ignored the bird's singing and remained on my bed. My son's presence made me feel uneasy. I didn't know what to do for his birthday. So I just did nothing. I posses no value, the only item I could call my own were the clothes I wore and Seven's gloves.

Rosaria pushed open the door. She was breathing heavily and her body was covered with sweat. She looked at me and said, in a nervous manner, "Chase has gone missing!

Seven and Rosaria remained in the house, just as I had ordered them to .I ran as fast as I could deeper and deeper into the forest. My wolf like hearing and sense of smell would make finding my son a quick and simple task. I prayed that I would find my son in good condition.

As I followed chase's sent, I noticed something strange. I noticed that his sent was leading me to a path that was familiar. His sent grew closer and closer, until we were separated by only a few feet. It was at that moment that I heard my son's horrifying scream. My heart was filled with so much fear.

"Where are you Chase", I said in discomfort. But there was only silence. Chase did not say a word. I followed his scent until it brought me to a clay hut. This was the home of the oracle.

"Chase, are you hear", I said with more discomfort.

It was quite for a moment then Chase replied, "Yes I'm here papa."

I walked in the hut slowly. The stench of the oracle still lingered. Chase sat beside the oracle's body, almost like he was taking care of her; taking care of the dead… how absurd.

"Chase, why did you come here", I demanded.

"It feels like I know her Papa", he began. "It looks like I'm too late to help her. I'm sorry if I scared anyone but it felt like no one could hear her shouting but me. She called out my name for help, so she must have known me… I couldn't just ignore her.

So…Chase has now made friends with my enemy. Things are happening in the oracle's favor. Soon Chase will become the most powerful of the oddity, and when that happens, I will be no more.

"Chase, my son", I said with a week voice. "Why did you scream earlier?"

"A snake was gonna eat me", he replied. "But Zeke killed the snake and rescued me". I searched around the room for the man known as Zeke, but all I could find was a baby white tiger. "Is this Zeke", I asked Chase, and he shook his head yes.

I carried my son and started walking home. He's growing up so fast now. "Happy birthday", I said to my son but had no gift for him. I felt another presence, as I turned around, I could see Zeke following use home.

"Can I keep him Papa", said Chase.

I felt guilty for not giving him a present so I gladly said yes. Zeke was now a part of the family; I wonder what my wife would think…

Seven and Rosaria waited in front of our home impatiently. Rosaria snatched Chase away from me and started beating him. Chase began crying immediately, but Rosaria continued, feeling that the lesson was not yet learned. It proved difficult for me to watch, so I turned away; but could still hear his cries. It was finally over, but the aftermath left two people weeping; a mother and a son.

Rosaria picked Chase up and squeezed him tightly. "You don't know how worried I was Chase", said Rosaria.

"I'm sorry mama", said Chase. "Don't be mad at me. I promise I won't do it again."

"Hush little one", Rosaria interjected.

She whipped the tears from her son's face and sang to him the song of emotions.

Chapter Seven

Love is Destructive

I wish to express my deepened admiration for the woman that rescued me from myself; I want to give thanks to the woman who filled my heart with so much kindness; kindness that I did not know existed outside a dream. This woman is my wife. For a reasonable amount of time she has been trying to teach me to write in her native language. But I'm afraid I'm not her most productive student. I want to give her a gift, something that will prove that I've acknowledged all that she's done for me. So I searched for a pen and paper and wrote down the words that my lips so scarcely spoke. I handed my wife the paper with a heavy heart. She read the Zodant words I wrote on the paper, then smiled at me and said "I love you too".

I woke up early the next morning and rushed to Seven's room. "Seven", I said silently.

I want to buy my wife a wedding ring. It will serve as an image of love's declaration. Without a ring our love seems like a pretense."

"I'm shocked that it took you this long to ask", said Seven. "Take my motor cycle and head east to Mute City. There you'll find a jewelry store. Take whatever bit of money I have left in my wallet. Money never brought me happiness anyway."

I hopped on the motor cycle and headed east, just as Seven

instructed. The sky was blue on this day. The sun shined brightly; and the forest was calm and tranquil. As time passed I saw fewer and fewer trees, until I made it to my final destination. Mute City, the great city of silence, amazing was the only word fit to describe it. This city is home to millions of people. The buildings grew like trees, until they pierced the heavens. As I drove into this laborite, I noticed that my presence had drawn the attention of several citizens, who knew about the power that the gloves I wore possessed.

I came across a jewelry store after hours of search. I got off the motor cycle and walked inside the jewelry store. The cashier seemed to be distracted willingly. It was clear that she didn't want to speak to me. I began searching for Rosaria's wedding ring by myself, until I saw one ring that caught my eye. That ring had a medium sized diamond complemented by lovely flower decorations. This was the perfect ring.

I approached the teenager once again and requested that she remove the wedding ring from its glass container. But my words couldn't be heard. So I just stood there as she flipped through her gossip magazine and chewing her gum like a hungry goat. She soon grew tired of my persistence, and brought the ring out of its container and snatched the money out of my hand so scornfully.

There was a sea of people waiting for me outside. Their eyes filled with both fear and hate. They were talking silently amongst themselves. Before things could get hostile, a cherry flavored sports car intervened. The doors slid up and a well dressed man in a white tuxedo stepped out. He had short brown hair and was of the same age as me. I could see that he also wore a glove with holes from the knuckles to the elbow.

"Hey, what's your name", demanded the man. His appearance was threatening, and he seemed to have the respect of the crowd. I was surrounded. And my enemy grew nearer. I stuffed the ring into my back pocket and after a silent prayer; prepared myself for battle. He now stood face to face to me, and he asked again "who are you?"

"My name is Reece Vega", I replied.

"My name is Johnny Sage", the man replied. I'm one of the soldiers in the new oddity. I'm recruiting men so we can put an end to Felix Crown's rule. You would be a good asset for our team.

"I'm not interested", I replied abruptly. I've come such a long way, now my life is of meaning. I don't want to lose all that I've obtained so; abstinence is the safest course of action.

"Understood", said Johnny. Those unyielding scares make your body a product of war. Luck has allowed you to elude death several times, even though you're a neutralist. When your luck runs out, as it's sure to do; you can always call on me.

He handed me a see through stone and I looked at it with confusion. He then tried to clarify things. "You put it in one of the holes on your glove. When this is done then you can call for help by simply screaming out the person's name. When you call for someone you set up a warp gate which brings the person to your location."

I did just as he said and put the stone inside one of the holes in my glove then bid him fair well. I hopped back on the motorcycle and drove away with the wedding ring safely stashed in my back pocket. The sun began to set as I exited mute city, making the journey home a dark and eerie one.

As I grew closer home I noticed that there was a shining light in front of my house. Rosaria, Zeke, Chase, and Seven were all missing. I walked inside my house and noticed a strange figure searching through the drawers and closets. I used the fire stone to create a small ball of light, which revealed the creature's identity. The creature was a strange mixture between man and reptile. Its head was red while the rest of its body was green. I punched the lizard man and the impact sent him flying through the wall. I picked him off the ground, and then started chocking his scaly neck demanding that he tell me where my family was. He then pointed to the shining light.

I prayed for my mother's courage and then leaped into the shining light.

I was transferred to a place much too familiar. I was in a storage room, and near me was an elevator. My family stood in the center of the room. I ran up to them to make sure everyone was well.

"Reece, I'm glad you could make it", said a familiar voice. I turned towards the voice's origin and could see Felix, Panic and Reece at the corner of the room. It now became clear where I was, the iron bison; the space ship that I was born in… and where my mother was taken away from me.

"Reece", said Rosaria. "You have a twin?"

"You seem pretty attached to them", said Felix. "If you want them alive then you better answer my questions sincerely."

I nodded my head in compliance.

"Such a reasonable man" said Felix. "Now tell me Reece, where is Leader-one's glove?"

"Leader-one", I thought to myself. "The name sounded familiar. As I recalled he was the leader of the original oddity. But he passed away over fifty years ago. I have no ties with that man, so how would I know where he hid his glove?"

I looked at him and then replied, "I don't know where the glove is."

"Wrong answer", said Panic.

He then brought out a gun, aimed it at my son, and then cocked it. "This is the last time I'm going to ask you," said Felix.

Rosaria squeezed Chase tightly and told him to look away from the red laser that pointed at his head.

"Please stop this", I begged.

"Where is Leader-one's glove", he repeated, this time more impatiently.

I did not know what to say. I told him the truth but he didn't believe me. I would have lied to him had I not feared the consequences. So I opened my mouth and answered again; "I don't know where it is."

Bang! Panic released the bullet as it set coarse to clam the life of my son, but Rosaria pushed Chase out of the way, substituting her own life.

I was in disbelief; devastated, overwhelmed by the simple fact that I had lost the person who gave me a reason to survive. In just a fraction of a second, this tiny bullet had undone all that I've worked so hard to achieve. It wasn't her time. Her life was stolen!

A pool of fire swarmed around me, my eyes turned red, my hands turned into claws.

"Seven you and Chase must get out of here", I demanded. "You're not gunna like what you see!"

Seven and Chase ran into the shining light with Rosaria's motionless body. "It's time", I commanded. All the long suppressed hatred I cared was dying to be released. And the wolf inside me forced its way out, like a bird emerging from its shell.

Panic threw his handgun to the side and slowly; confidently, thinking that nothing had changed since our last encounter. I waited until he was close enough, and then stomped hard on the ground. A wall of fire circled me. Panic was caught in the circle and the dancing flames rendered his body helpless for a short period of time. I used this time to my advantage and punched him to the ground.

Felix; in disappointment with Panics performance, substituted Panic with an army of Lizard men. There were well over a hundred of them; each just as ugly as the last, crawling out of every dark corner, like roaches.

It was me against an army, there was no way I could beat all of them. Continuing this fight was suicide. It was then that I recalled what Johnny Sage said to me when I was in Mute City, about how the stone he had given me could be used to activate a warp gate.

I screamed out the name "Sage" and a shining light emerged behind me. Johnny Sage stepped out from within the light. He wore a large brown coat and sun glasses. He remained calm and was not at all bothered by our enemies' number. Johnny threw down his coat and revealed two automatics strapped to his leg, a high caliber handgun on his waist, a shotgun on the opposite waist side, a rifle on is back, along with a large weapon which looked like a cannon. He began to shoot down our enemies one by one with the rifle. The bullet pierced through their scaly bodies and killed on contact. When the rifle ran out of ammunition, he threw it to the ground and reached for the automatics. He sprayed its bullets across the room; with so many foes every shot was guaranteed, so he didn't even bother to aim. He threw down his weapon, since it ran out of bullets, and then brought out his shotgun to do away with the final lizard man. The battle ended in a matter of seconds. He dropped his final weapon, leaving behind empty bullets and magazines where he stood. He approached the warp gate, but before he left he looked at me and said, "Now do you understand." The warp gate then closed behind him.

I looked around the room and saw that the warp gate that I had came from was closing as well. I turned back into a man and walked in before it closed. The warp gate took me back home. Seven, Chase, and Zeke were all gathered around Rosaria's lifeless body.

I approached my wife slowly and noticed that she wasn't breathing. I sat by her side then shook her body gently.

"Wake up Rosaria", I instructed. "C'mon! Please get up. Get up Rosaria, speak to me.

My eyes filled with tears as I shook her body more. "Let me hear your voice! Say something… anything! For god's sake, please, don't leave me. I need you now more than ever. Let me hear your voice! Let me hear your voice."

I dug my fingers into my pocket and removed the ring I had bought for her. "Seven gave me some money today. I used it to buy you a ring from Mute City; it was gunna be a surprise, that's why I was gone so long. If I had known this would have happen I would have never left your side."

I slide it on her finger. "Rosaria… will you marry me?"

There was no answer. The silence grew. More tears ran down my face. I embraced her dearly, never wanting to be apart. Both our bodies were stained with blood. I hated myself for not being able to save her. I wished I could go back in time for just a moment. All of this could have been undone.

I dug up a hole near our home and buried my wife in it. As I turned around I noticed that Chase was also crying, but there was nothing I could do. Even the song of emotions couldn't repair this damage. It rained on this day, just like when my mother died. I got back on the motorcycle and made a vow never to love again. Too often have I witnessed love's destruction.

"Where are you going", said Seven.

"To kill Felix Crown", I replied

Chapter Eight

Belly of the Beast

The road to Mute City seemed even longer than before and the night became as dark as the mood that I'd felt. I indulged in the pleasure of revenge until I arrived in the great city of silence. I felt like a deadly weapon, cocked and loaded, all I needed was someone to show me my opponent.

I shouted the name "Sage" and a warp gate appeared. Johnny Sage stepped out of the shining light as promised.

"What seems to be the problem", he said.

"Where can I find Felix Crown", I demanded.

He paused, and examined the anguish in my eyes.

"Felix never leaves the Iron Bison", he began. "In addition to that he is a native from a tribe called Mythica, the glove he wears grants him immortality. When Eugene Osco created the first Oddity he tried to replicate the DNA of a native. The power glove recognizes the Oddity as a native, but fortunately we can remove it at will. Should you be a pure native, the glove will become entwined with your flesh until the day you die and your flesh withers away."

"So what you're saying is that there's no point in fighting", I interjected.

"I didn't say that", he began. "Do you think the natives are ignorant enough to create a weapon that can give a mad man immortality? There are three dominant gloves, one from the Mythicans, and another from the Zodants, and the last from the Coralian. Each glove has its weakness, as a form of balance. The Mythican glove dominates the Coralian, the Coralian glove dominates the Zodant, and the Zodant dominates the Mythican. The only glove that can beat Felix's is the one from the Zodant tribe, which is best known as Leader-one's glove."

I then recalled Felix Crown's demand when I was inside the Iron Bison.

"Where is Leader-One's glove", I questioned.

"I don't know", replied Johnny. My guess is that a member of the original Oddity, or someone who understood the importance of that balance simply hid it."

"Seven", I thought to myself.

"What if I was to find the location of the glove", I questioned.

"Alone, Felix poses too much of a threat. Even with the glove we would still have to worry about those that support Felix, like Panic, the original Reece Vega, and the Panoptic bruiser. But if they were out of the picture..."

"Then our odds of winning would increase", I interjected. "Where can I find Panic?"

"Panic is in North Tower while the Bruiser is in a Tower to the East", said Sage. "We have a common enemy. Together we can crush our opponent. But the anguish in your eyes tells me that you'd rather fight alone."

"Yes, he is the one to blame for my wife's death. He must die by my hands alone. The same can be done to the Bruiser.

"No", said Johnny. "The bruiser is mine."

I followed the map that Johnny gave me and it led me straight to North Tower. As I drove closer I noticed that there was a large number of people surrounding the tower. I got off my motorcycle and was making my way to the entrance when the guards blocked my path.

"Where do you think you're going", he demanded.

I looked around and noticed that they were all armed.

"When I ask you a question I expect an answer immediately", he said impatiently.

"Allow me to pass", I said.

My demand forced the guards into a drunken laughter. I hated being laughed at. As time went by their laughter seized and one of the guards tried to restore order.

"I recommend you turn around and run away while you're still breathing", said another guard.

But I wasn't affected by his hollow threats so I asked again, "allow me to pass and I will spear your life."

They all made their weapons visible, and circled around me like wild dogs moving in for the kill. One of the guards swung at me with a bat, I dodged the first swing and caught the bat when he swung again. I snapped it in two and threw it to the ground. They all attacked me at once, and I created an inferno, severely burning everything around me. Now there was no one to stop me from reaching the entrance.

Inside the North Tower was filled with more wild dogs; each wanting to get their hands on the intruder. I threw fire at every guard in site, and then watched as the flames danced. There was only one guard remaining but he ran like an animal from wildfire, until he trapped himself in a corner. He was frozen with fear. I walked toward the guard confidently; he shook violently, then pulled the alarm that hung on the wall, fearing for his life.

"Your too late", said the terrified guard. "Now everyone in North Tower knows you're here, including Panic."

I grabbed him by the neck then pulled him towards me until our noses almost touched and whispered "good, you saved me the trouble".

"Just like snapping a toothpick", I said while walking into an elevator. I traveled to the highest floor on the tower. I had a strange feeling that I would find Panic there. The elevator stopped… but something was odd. My wolf-like hearing was picking up heavy breathing, unsynchronized. There were dozens of guards waiting for me just passed the elevator doors. I jumped to the roof of the elevator, and then held on to the steel woven rope. Before the door could open all the way, hundreds of bullets forced their way into the elevator walls, while others were scattered randomly on the ground. If I had remained in the elevator I would have been dead. This close encounter with death was evidence that Felix Crown's advocates should not be taken likely. I waited until the guards ran out of ammunition, and the piercing shells came to a halt. One of the guards stepped cautiously into the elevator to collect my remains. But there was nothing there.

"This area is clear", he said; relieved by his discovery.

I jumped off the roof and pounced down on my enemy. He laid unconsciously on the floor. The crashing sound was heard by the other guards, but the gun smoke greatly limited one's visibility. I then ran out of the smoke and slashed the remaining guards with my claws. They fell to the ground leaving behind a trail of red paint.

There was a huge door on that floor. This was the room where Panic would be. Those guards were his last line of defense. I swung the door open and asserted my way in. it was dark inside the room. I couldn't even see the hands in front of my face.

"I'm surprised you made it this far", said a voice in the darkness.

"Show yourself Panic", I demanded. "Hiding in the shadows won't protect you much longer."

The lights turned on, and I could see Panic hanging from the roof like a bat. He jumped off the roof and landed in front of me, shaking the ground beneath me.

"You look like a strong fighter", said Panic, while standing only a few inches away from me. "But the original Reece Vega could kill me in a few seconds. So how about we make this a little bit more interesting? There is a bomb in this room that's set to blow up in one minute. All exits are sealed, that means you won't have a place to run away to this time. Only I know the code to defuse the bomb and you have to beat me to get it. This is a simple task for the real Reece Vega; let's see how his imposter compares. You only have forty-nine seconds remaining."

"Forty-nine seconds remaining", I said smiling intimidating. "That's all the time I need. You have no idea what you're up against."

I tripped him and he fell to the ground hard, but got up just as quickly. I ran towards him and tried to kick him back down, but he grabbed my foot and flung me into the wall. There were only twenty-five seconds remaining. I spat fire at my enemies, then I withdrew my attack in fear that it would set off the bomb. Panic closed his eyes and tried to shield his body with his hands. Only sixteen seconds remained. I punched him as hard as I could and he fell to the ground. Panic's knees weekend and he stumbled to stay on two feet. His shirt had burnt away, reveling the scar I had given him. I lifted him up by the neck then bashed my head into his. He fell to his knees. I turned my hands into claws and prepared to deliver the final blow when I realized that I needed the code to disarm the bomb.

"Panic", I yelled.

"Admit defeat and give me the code."

Panic laughed menacingly then looked into my eyes and said, "I would rather die than to see you live another day."

Only five seconds remained. I tried opening the door I had came from but it was sealed. Only four seconds remained... how am I going to get out! Three seconds remained... C'mon Reece think. Two seconds remained... I'm running out of time. One second remained, Panic said he sealed all exits but he forgot one. Zero...

I jumped out of the window before it was too late. I was now concerned about surviving the ten thousand feet drop. I charged up my fire energy, and then shot a beam of fire to the ground that broke my fall. Never had I been so happy to touch soil before. I walked away calmly.

"The nightmare is finally over", I said to myself.

I then heard a crashing sound behind me. I turned around slowly and then approached the figure; there laid Panic's motionless body.

"How do you feel Panic", I questioned boastfully. "The overwhelming pain of loss is bottled up inside of you; that and the simple thought that no matter how hard you try you cannot defeat your enemies. You are helpless; I can bully your life, and take all that you hold dear. The tables have turned! Now you know how I've felt my whole life; you heartless pig!"

I began to punch his dead body. And then he awoke!

"Did you think you were the only one", he questioned, as I cringed in a nervous confusion.

"How is he still alive", I questioned myself. "He fell from thousands of feet, how the hell do you live through that!?"

"Did you think you were the only one with the gift? I have to admit it made me a bit arrogant at first when I used it. I allowed you to have your moment, I allowed you to transform into that beast and growl around the battle field as if you were something special. In truth, you're no different from the rest of us. Now, let me show you what true power is."

Panic's skin turned gray like concrete, his muscles expanded, his eyes turned red and a large horn grew from his forehead. He had transformed his body into a rhino. He leaped into the air and pounced down on my body. It felt like two tunes came crashing into me. His tremendous weight made it impossible to breath. I tried my best to knock him off of me, but it failed. I laid on the ground at the receiving end of his punches gasping for air like a fish out of water. He lifted me above his shoulders and punched me to the ground. I got up as quickly as possible, I rushed up to him and punched him once in the stomach. My fist bruised as I hit him. I yelled from the pain. He laughed at my attack's inability to harm him. Fear surrounded me. I backed away from him until my back touched North Tower. The Rhino came charging at me. His horn pierced into my stomach and came out my back. I covered the hole with my hand, trying to stop the bleeding. Panic roared with laughter; the pain grew stronger by the second. At this moment I felt like all hopes of winning this battle were lost. He beat me again!

"No, no, I can't die", I said to myself.

"Not here, not by his hands, not with her death un-avenged. This is not my bitter end...!

My hands turned into claws, black hairs grew all around my body, my eyes turned red. I had become the wolf once again. I used my claws and pierced through his rock hard skin. He bled from the attack.

I leaped on top of his shoulders and drilled my piercing teeth into his skull, then viciously dragged it left to right. He died a bloody death. I whipped the blood from my mouth then turned back into a human. I could see Johnny Sage approaching me from a distance. I fell to the ground, unconscious; do to the massive blood lose. I was lying next to Panic, we both appeared dead.

Chapter Nine

The Great Destroyer

"Am I dead", I questioned myself.

"No", responded an old man in a lab coat. "But you were very close to it. My name is Dr. Eugene Osco II."

"Dr. Osco", I repeated. "Your father was responsible for creating the Oddity, correct?"

"Yes", responded Osco. "My father was a great man. Humanity exists due to his perseverance and ingenuity.

I made an attempt to get off the bed but felt such a tremendous amount of pain which forced me to submission.

Johnny walked in the room with a blank look on his face.

"I underestimated my opponent", I said to him. "I'm not fit to fight the bruiser now."

"Your luck to be alive", he said that o so familiar phrase.

"The Bruiser is mine alone", he interrupted; and then walked out the door.

I've never seen this side of him before, so irrational. Who is the Panoptic Bruiser and what kind of hold did he have on Sage? I couldn't help but to wonder.

"The Bruiser is the man responsible for the death of Johnny's family", Osco began.

"Though the obituary states that his family is deceased, he still believes that his brother, Jason Sage, is still alive. I suppose it is a man's intuition, if you will. Every night he walks the streets like a ghost, searching for his brother. The bruiser made Johnny sage the man that he is today, and Johnny hates him for that. The Bruiser must die by his hands alone."

"I understand", I replied. I too have lost someone very meaningful to me. I made my way off the bed and requisitioned some clothing from Sage's wardrobe and then asked Osco if the wealthy Johnny Sage could lend me a motorcycle. He tried to persuade me that I was in a poor physical condition, but my persistence made it a losing battle. My goal was to travel to the Trinity Apartment Complex, where my mother and I once lived; there I'd hope to regain pieces of my memory.

I saw a skinny man standing in the rain, just outside the mansion. This man had short, neatly groomed blond hair that was brushed back. He had blue eyes and wore skinny blue jeans with a tight leather jacket. As I examined him closer I noticed that he also wore a power glove.

"My name is Vince Mansheeno", said the skinny man. "I am part of the new Oddity as well."

I tried to sustain my laughter. Vince seemed so week, so fragile; how could he assist us. I introduced myself to him and walked away so discourteously.

As I drove to the Trinity Apartment Complex, I saw construction workers beating down the building. I was powerless, and found myself watching as they reduced my former home to rubble. I thought I would find happiness here but all I see is more destruction. I then felt a needle piercing into my neck. Alarmed, I quickly reached to the back of my neck and removed it. It was a tranquilizer.

I was soon surrounded by police cars. The sirens amplified as the police cars grew closer. Dozens of police cars drove up to me, coming from every direction. Not only was I out numbered, severely injured, but the tranquilizer was taking effect. I caught a glimpse of Vince Mansheeno before I fell to the ground. He watched anxiously from a distance with a smile on his face. They took away my glove, then shoved me to the back seat and sent me on a one way trip to the penitentiary.

I do not deserve this punishment. The marshals accused me of being someone called the Great Destroyer. I was convinced that Vince had framed me. But the guards and prisoners believed that he and I are one in the same. I was giving a life sentence for the random bombings around Mute City. I would rot away in this jail cell. If I had my glove I could break out of this prison with ease. Without my glove I felt week, but when I wear it every one respects me like a gun. That respect was gone forever.

Most of the prisoners had already given up hope. But there were a handful of prisoners who had the will to live. I admired these prisoners. Every month, on visiting days, they would be visited by friends and family. The guards loved to beat down on those kinds of prisoners. That's why I forced myself to maintain this rugged posture; I refused to be broken down. They see me as the great destroyer, but in truth, I was dying on the inside while my exterior appeared fearless.

I had no family to come and visit me. I wondered how my son was doing. I thought about my wife. The wedding ring only brought tears to my eyes. I looked around my cage and tried to tell myself that it'll be alright. My lips were closed but my mind remained wide open.

I later overheard one of the guards talk about my glove being in the guards cabin. The glove that gave me so much strength was only a few feet away. I needed to think of a way out of this place, but how? Escape was impossible. The guards forced us to wear ankle weights that no man could break, they carried weapons that no man could jump through, and they built huge fences that no man could jump past. But there was one thing that the guards failed to understand; Reece Vega was no ordinary man. I used my wolf characteristics to take back my gloves and break out of that prison.

Chapter Ten

Regret

"Where the hell is he", I demanded as I walked into Sage's mansion.

"Where is Vince Mansheeno? That arrogant bastard accused me of being the great destroyer and forced me to captivity."

"Calm down Reece", said Johnny.

"That loathsome individual abandoned us. But before he left he told me that you no longer wish to be part of the Oddity, and I believed him too; recalling your lone wolf and independent nature. But right now we have bigger things to worry about. Felix is mimicking Dr. Osco's work, and trying to create his own breed of emotionless super solders. If he proves successful, then his dreams of becoming mankind's eternal overseer will be realized. We must destroy the iron bison and project Oddity while its still incomplete."

"Leader-one's gloves", he paused.

"Do you still remember where it is?"

This question caught me off guard. I've been gone for so long. He didn't bother to look for me, but the first thing he asks is for that glove.

"Yes", I replied. "I still remember where it is; it's… home"

I borrowed another motorcycle from Johnny Sage. And then I

traveled along that familiar path. It was dark when I arrived. Five cruel years have passed since I last returned home. But everything looked the same… unchanged by the flow of time. Even Rosaria's grave resembled how it once was. I approached the front door then opened it slowly. It was at this moment when a shadowy figure leaped down from the neighboring trees and struck me with a stick. The stick snapped in two as soon as it made contact.

"Take another step and it will be your last", said the figure.

As I turned around I could see a poorly dressed boy accompanied by a tiger.

"Chase", I said with uncertainty.

"Chase is that you? You've grown so much since I last saw you. Chase… what's the matter boy don't you recognize me? It's me Papa.

He examined me closely, from head to toe.

"Dad", he questioned.

"Is it really you this time? Are my eyes playing tricks on me again? I thought I would never see you again."

"Tell me Chase, where is Seven?"

"Seven has fallen ill", replied Chase.

"He is not strong like he once was. He just lies in bed all day… can't even feed himself."

I walked into the wooden house, and Chase followed closely behind. I made my way to Seven's room and could see him lying motionless on his bed. I was then greeted by the stench of a rotten corpse. He had been dead for just over a week.

Chase then walks towards Seven's lifeless body and wraps him in a blanket.

"Its cold outside", he began.

"I don't want grandpa to catch a cold. Grandpa needs his sleep so he can grow strong again."

"You must listen to me Chase! Did grandpa tell you where Leader-One's glove was, before he went to sleep?"

"Yes", he replied.

"He gave it to me as a gift. He said that it would protect me from danger, if I chose to wear it."

"I need you to give me the glove", I said.

"It's very important."

"It's been five years since you left", Chase began. This glove is the reason why you returned. If I give it to you then you will walk out of my life again, father; but this time you will have no reason to come back home."

"Give it here", I demanded. But Chase just stood still and looked to the ground. I needed that glove. Revenge was so important to me. The Oracle said that someday my son would be the strongest out of all of use. With that in mind, against his will, I forced my son to wear the glove of the Zodant trib.

"It won't come off", Chase shouted hysterically.

Upon further observation, I noticed that the glove had intertwined with his flesh. I then recalled the rules, which precede these gloves. Those of native blood could never remove the glove; Chase had obviously inherited the jeans from his mother. Chase would have to wear those gloves for the rest of his life. It was horrific to see him crying on the ground, struggling to rip off his own hands.

Large gusts of wind suddenly appeared and the trees and grass all bowed away from its presence. As I looked to the sky I saw a large air craft descending. It was Johnny Sage. I dragged Leader-One's gloves into the air craft, and he wept, and sobbed, then took his eyes to the window to watch his best friend Zeke growing further away.

"We can't leave Zeke Papa", he said to me as the air craft floated away, taking use to our final fight.

We approached the Iron Bison; the place of my creation. Johnny landed the air craft inside a storage department, and then forced his way into a nearby elevator. Chase and I followed. The elevator came to a halt and left us in a familiar room.

"There is no one here", I said in confusion.

"Johnny, use this to your advantage and begin detonating the ship."

Johnny did not respond. It was at that moment when I felt the thrust of a dagger being pierced into my back. The dagger left a hole in the same place that Panic had. I used my hands to try and stop the bleeding. As I turned around I could see Johnny holding a bloody dagger.

"Why have you betrayed me", I questioned.

Johnny roared with an evil laugh, "I think it's about time I end this Charade."

He then changed into a man that I had never seen before. This man wore a long black robe and his face was painted white and black.

"A shape shifter", I said in overwhelming pain.

"I am the Panoptic Bruiser", said the shape shifter.

"Felix Crown's most faithful advocate. My lord ordered me to do away with the new resistance Oddity and locate the glove from the Zodant tribe. I have divided your comrades; alone the Oddity is like a wasp without its stinger. In addition, you have delivered to me the keeper of Leader-One's glove. Perish the thought of victory, and bow down to the merciless master."

The bruiser pointed to the other side of the storage room, and there stood Felix Crown and the original Reece Vega. I was truly in bad company. With nothing to say to me, Felix waved his hand as if holding a baton; and released a horde of deadly lizard men. I was wounded, and the lizard men all pounced on me; chewing away my flesh like vultures or some breed of scavenger. They slashed my body relentlessly with their claws, not satisfied until their hands and mouth was filled with human blood.

"Stop it", my son demanded as he rushed to my rescue during a time in which I felt ever so helpless. Alone my little boy battled away a deadly army.

"Behold the power of Leader-One's glove", said Felix with a smirk.

Explosion's occurred within the Iron Bison and the space ship began to plunge to the ground, as if things were not bad enough. I had to find a way back to the ground. I tried to get on my feet but my body would not permit it; so then I crawled to the elevator, leaving behind a trail of blood.

"Chase", I called. But my words were submerged by the heat of battle. I called for his name again and an explosion replayed, serving as a reminder of how dire the situation was. I couldn't help my son, my body was damn near immobile, and so I made a difficult decision and pressed the elevator up.

When I reached the top I was driven insane with deep regret. My son saved my life, and in return I left him alone with the deadliest faces on this planet. As I reached to press down a figure dragged me by my neck out of the elevator. He clasped his two hands so tightly around my neck as he lifted me up and walked to the edge of the falling ship. My eyes demanded to know who this mysterious figure was, and it was none other than Vince Mansheeno.

"You blew up the ship didn't you", I questioned.

"Why are you doing this? We're on the same side!"

"I am something that most people could only dream of becoming", he began.

"I've seen you turn into that monster. I've looked into those demonic eyes and seen nothing but sin. I do the dirty work that society deem immoral. You're no good Reece Vega. I am the hero that advances God's schedule, the destroyer of evil, and no matter which side you claim to fight for, you cannot escape your due reckoning.

"It was you who sent me to jail," I said.

"You were the great destroyer all along."

He punched me down to the dark clouds without a care.

"I guess this is it", I thought as I plunged down thousands of feet in the air; and stretched out my hand for someone to hold, like a drowning child reaching out to be rescued. My body was in overwhelming pain, but still I found the strength to smile. I smiled because the Oracle's haunting words were of pure fiction, I hadn't died by the hands of my son; and I smiled because I would finally get to be with my wife again.

Chapter One

The Case of: Chase Vega

Grandpa was gone; Papa too. I wished that my mama was here. She always knew what to do, she provided a shoulder to lean on, and the words, I love you. Unfortunately, she has been gone the longest. The home that love built, now became a haunting reminisce of happy years. I had nothing that I could call my own, no one left to care for me. Everything that I held so dearly in this world had been eradicated! My life had been savagely ripped apart by death.

I wanted to curl into a ball and comfort myself; I wanted to touch my own flesh, but the damn glove wouldn't come off. I yelled frantically, and caused some physical damage to myself while trying to remove it. It was hopeless. I shook my head in disbelief and tried to tell myself that everything would be alright. I soon fell to my knees and whelped a heartfelt silhouette, as I realized the pretence of my very words. It seems that lately, all my heart has felt was pain, and I even went as far as to question god on the existence of a heart.

In time, my mind's eye discovered an image approaching closer and closer.

"They're here to finish me off", I thought to myself.

I was still curled into a ball, my life was held with little value; this intruder could do whatever he wanted to me. The intruder sat on the ground with me and licked my face.

"Zeke", I yelled in excitement.

I took in his very essence and then I closely embraced the last surviving member of my family.

"It's a good thing you didn't follow me into that ship", I said.

"You probably wouldn't have survived the accident."

Zeke's presence forced a smile. Some of the sadness was lifted but still I thought of my mother. I considered building a time machine so that I could return to the days when I was happy. I couldn't shake the way I felt. I wanted to hear her voice, embrace her and share the same air. My thoughts of her became obsessive, and only then did she return to me…

"Mama", I called with tearful eyes.

She stood barefooted under the moonlight, wearing the slippery velvet colored dress that she was murdered in. Her skin was pail, almost ghostly.

"This is a dream come true", I said as I gave a visceral sprint to embrace my mother.

She stretched out her hand to touch my own. I let go of all my tragedy and stretched out my hand to touch her. It was then that I noticed her, sort of, drifting away from me as I got closer. I ran as fast as I could but I still couldn't keep up. She was just an arm's length away. I ran for miles through the dangerous forest to touch my image of boundless pleasure. She slipped further and further away from me, until she became just a fading glimmer of light drifting into the unknown. In bitter frustration, I could do nothing but follow the path that I believed she could have drifted along.

My blind search led me toward a romantic sea shore. It offered a comforting breeze and the relaxing sand beneath my feet was much needed. I complied with the ambient sound of nature. I had never wondered too far from my home, so all these sensations were very new to me. It was all so amazing to me.

My pursuit for my mother had left me dehydrated. I scooped some of the ocean water into the palm of my hands. I had a sip of it and then spat it out almost immediately.

"The water tasted like tears", I said to myself.

"Come on Zeke, lets continue our search elsewhere."

Together we marched along Mother's presumed coarse. The number of trees slowly diminished as we made our way out of the forest. We came across a dirt road and instinctively followed, believing that it may have been Mother's path. In time I found myself tiring from thirst and hunger. My feet grew wiry; I had been walking for hours.

I heard a noise coming from the bushes which grew parallel to the dirt road. I diverted my attention to the source and then I armed myself with a stick from a nearby tree; I had no idea what I would find...a rabbit emerged from the bushes.

Without hesitation, I quickly caved to mortal needs and swung the stick voraciously at the defenseless creature. The creature squirmed helplessly on the ground. Red blood gushed from the animal's scull. My hand... my glove was stained with blood. I swung again and again, creating a pool of blood around the animal. I raised my hand to deliver the final blow and the creature's eyes locked into my own. In its eyes I saw overwhelming pain and sorrow, all of which I had caused. I lessened my grip on the stick, and then let go.

"What have I done", I thought to myself.

I stood next to the rabbit; crying. My warm tears rinses its blood stained fur. The animal was barely alive but in seconds it would comply with death.

It was then that I learned something without having it thought to me. I became aware of the glove's special ability instinctively; leader-One's glove allowed me to steal pain and suffering from another living creature. With no time to waist, I closed my eyes and touched the dying creature. The rabbit's pain slowly flowed into my body; I began to bleed, my bones became fractured and I passed out from the pain.

As I woke the next morning, I noticed that I was unscathed. The animal, along with the pool of blood had vanished. But Zeke stayed by my side as always. He had even hunted down a deer to settle our noisy stomach. At first I felt sympathy for this dead animal, but I came to realize that for something to survive something else most be sacrificed.

I rose to my feet and greeted the rising sun. We continued our search for mother like two lost souls, until we reached the end of the road; and thru the rocky down curve laid the spell binding beauty of Mute City. I looked at this giant ant colony with amazement!

"This must be where mother ran away to", I thought to myself.

There was no time for lateness! I ran to the city with an open eye and an eager heart. I couldn't wait to see her again. This time... I'm going to keep her all to myself.

The roads were filled with angry drivers who were impeded by heavy traffic. The streets flared with frustration. On the sidewalks were hordes of busy civilians who were left under the same inconvenience.

"Excuse me sir", I interrupted.

"Have you seen my Mother?"

Some did not bother to stop; others casted me to the side, along with my thoughts.

"Excuse me", I restated upon a more likely candidate. But of course I received the same response. I tried from sun rise to sunset, but it seemed like nobody had time for me. After all, I was just a child.

I searched for a place where Zeke and I could sleep and was fortune enough to find an abandoned alley. It was; however, along the more dangerous areas of the city, where five-fingered monsters roamed freely. Heartless criminals standing around every corner... plotting there next big hit. The walls were covered with drawings and colorful writings. The streets were filled with trash and may hem; it wasn't a shock why the law enforcement officers refused to patrol this part of the city.

"Hey kid, are you lost", they would question.

The gloves in which I was forced to wear made my strength unmatched. I came here in the name of love; I could not be easily threatened. In the city's carnage, I ruled.

Zeke and I gathered some cardboard boxes, anything we found laying around, and build a home in that abandoned alley. Our home was unavailing to most people. But to me it was our secret construct in which no one may intrude. We laid our weary heads and prepared for tomorrow's search for mother.

The street light casted a shadow of me on the wall; I gazed at it and imagined it to be a blueprint of myself. It was then that I noticed my shadow moving on its own will. "It was coming to life", I thought to myself. I turned my head and saw that Zeke was fast asleep and blind to this phenomenon. My shadow grew two giant moonlike eyes and lashed out its hands towards me. The creature pierced into my soul and laughed like a child.

"Who are you", I fearfully demanded.

"I am Chase Vega", he replied.

"That can't be", I thought to myself. "Then who am I?"

"You are Chase Vega as well", he replied.

"I am the realization of the image that lives far beneath your subconscious mind. You and I are two different entities sharing a common sociological identifier. I am the shroud of moral fiber, which resides in your darkest dreams; you brought me to life. As a reflection of thyself, I too have witnesses your loneliness. The tragedy that surrounds you has, unfortunately, shaped the very content of your heart. I wish to liberate the true identity restrained in the core of your subjective thoughts."

"I don't understand what you're talking about", I said. "Nothing is making sense to me."

He paused and then began again.

"Human organs, like the mind and heart are made of brittle components; delicate like flower, and fragile like glass. Though it may prove to be unbearable at times you must understand that all hearts feel pain so easily. All living things feel pain and it is the embracement of this pain which makes us all fundamentally the same. Put yourself in the company of others, for those inaccurate self portraits will someday serve as the heart's advocate. Humans are beings of constant change.

Your greatest fear, like most people, is the ever present thought of being hated. You don't want to let down those you love. You don't want people to interpret your actions negatively. As a result you find yourself constantly begging for others to make decisions for you. By doing so, you abandon responsibility and elude the bitter self hatred that may precede error. This instinctive reflex makes it impossible to live alone; this is the position in which you are placed in today. A hopeless and delusional search serves as the reason for your existence. What is it that you truly wish for? It's quite clear that you love your mother, but do you love yourself?

Chapter Two

The Juveniles

"Just twenty seconds until they arrive", I said to myself as I waited in the Center of an empty playground. I was alone, sitting, smiling.

"They will be here soon", I kept telling myself. "The bell will release them all, just as it has before. I turned my neck in response to the ringing bell; here they come!

They took shape like an army ascending from the horizon. They stampeded toward me, shouting, omitting their unique state of being. They were so violently happy. They ran towards me like a flock of radiant birds, bestowed with the gift of absolute freedom. Their presence pierced me sharply!

"The juveniles have arrived", I said to myself.

One of the Juveniles ferociously tackled me into the sand. He laid on top of me, his body weight nearly crushed my own. I struggled to brush the dirt from my face. Triumphantly, the Juveniles rose their voice to say, "What game do you want to play today Chase?"

I can truly say that their intentions have always been pure. These Juveniles; these elementary school children were clasped by their common, playful, thrill-seeking desire. I became a member of their sacred doctrine.

"What game do you want to play today," said the Juveniles.

"I know, lets play tag," said another Juvenile.

"Let's see who can swing the highest," said another.

"Let's have a race down the big slide," another interjected.

"Let's play on the monkey bars", another began.

"No, let's dig a really big hole.

The juveniles created a world of joyful freedom, pleasure; warmth. They created a world in which every living thing fortunate enough to touch its path was overwhelmed by love. It was such a simple yet complex way of living.

"Let's just play, let's just have fun", they would often say.

They ignored all problems outside of the playground and simply cared for each other. I understood that the ways of these children would persist as long as the earth and the sun allowed. There advanced way of life was eternal. When one Juvenile grows, and goes about his or her separate way, the next generation will bring more Juveniles to carry on the sacred doctrine.

The parents came to the playground to pick up their children. The parents who ran on a less flexible schedule would tear the Juvenile from their sacred rituals. Other's who's schedules permitted wouldn't dare disturb the child's innocent laughter. Unfortunately, the amount of Juveniles fell with the descending sun. We decided to play one final game of baseball before we bid our farewells. The patience of those parents with a flexible schedule was put to the test. But that's just the way the Juveniles were; always asking for one more game. The parents sat on the bleachers near the baseball field. They cheered uncontrollably when it came time for their Juvenile to bat.

"Way to go, that's my boy", they would say.

The bleachers grew silent when it came time for me to bat. There was no one to root me on. I looked back at the bleachers and nearly burst to tears.

The sun was gone; all of the Juveniles too. I sat alone on the swing with my head faced down; I was crying.

My shadow took shape on the swing nearest to me.

"What's the matter Chase", he questioned.

"I still haven't found where my happiness lies", I said while fighting back my tears.

"What do I do?"

I sincerely confessed that I was incapable of making my own decisions. With that said, I pleaded to him with an even greater desperation.

"Please tell me what I should do now", I demanded.

He didn't reply. Shadow wanted to teach me a lesson; to live on my own prohibitions and to feel no regret from mistakes in which I chose to learn from. It seemed a bit unreal for him to demand so much from me. After all, I was still just a kid.

Chapter Three

To the rescue

Ten years have gone by since I last returned to where the Juveniles played. I slowly grew into a state of inescapable depression. I began to hold my very own life with little value. I desperately searched thru every direction for my mother and in time, thoughts of finding mother began to differ. The sweet memories of yesterday, was washed away by a sea of loneliness.

If there is an omnipotent being who views and cradles' our precious lives, then my eternal heart ache should prove irrefutable evidence to give me back the one in which I truly desire.

I sat sleeplessly in the dark alley I called home. I was counting the numbers I scared into the walls. The glove's final ability came to me soon after I left the Juveniles. I received haunting visions of innocent people dying, ten minutes before it happened. I would do my best to save their lives; those innocent people. The lives of those I could not save were represented with a mark on the wall. These visions knew no limit. A vision of death would appear as I indulged in a beautiful dream, turning it into bona fide nightmare. The vision would impede on days purged with a celestial perfection.

Death of the innocent would overlap, so often; leaving me with the dilemma of choosing which perfect stranger deserved to live. I was at a loss of words as I gazed at the numbers on the wall. There were thousands...

It was then that another painful vision came to me! I closed my eyes to suppress the pain but then was awakened by a frantic scream. The vision occurred to me with such unimaginable ferocity. I became the eyes of the victim. I could hear them panting, drowning; no, suffocating. The walls were on fire. Yes, in the vision I sat with them as the flames and smoke grew tall. I sat with the mother and child as they shouted for help; but my image and hopeful words could not be recognized. They held each other so dearly as the flames grew dangerously near. I shut my eyes, like people do when cars collide. But I could still hear them screaming...

I opened my eyes; the vision was over. I was crying. The couple reminded me of a personal experience. I saw myself and my mother in that burning building.

I now had ten minutes to make a difference. I'll prevent this all from happening.

I rose to my feet and innately dashed to the section of the city where the tragic event would occur. At first I traveled along the roads and sidewalks, but soon found the crowded streets to be an impediment. I turned to the skies as an alternative route, scaling the tallest buildings and zigzagging rooftops with my unearthly speed. As I ran I kept a strong emphasis on time. My body was drenched in sweat, my legs felt as if they had gained a tremendous amount of weight, and my brittle lungs had collapsed so long ago. I was at a loss of oxygen; dizzy, light headed. I wished that I could stop and rest, but I knew those seconds lost could be life costing. I replayed the events of my vision over and over again. My body was running on reserve power now, fueled only by the strength of my iron will.

The smoke filled sky complemented my nearness. I was panting like some over worked slay dog. On the very next building, were the blaring flames of imminent danger. Nestled in the core of the hostile inferno were the virtuous mother and child. I was near there company, but the building I stood on retreated approximately fifty five yards from my desired destination. I back stepped toward the edge of the roof, and then ran with all my might towards the opposing frontier. I gave a visceral leap in hopes of clearing a fifty five yard air space. My heart was with fear, I didn't know whether to keep my eyes closed or open. If I didn't make this jump I would surely die. I decided to close my eyes as my body crashed against the sharp glass window. The sound of my body slamming against the building amplified the pain. I opened my eyes to witness blood and glass fragments laying all around me. This did not comfort the pain at all. My heart rate increased dramatically and my lungs found the smoke filled building to harbor insufficient oxygen.

I was soon introduced by a child's spell binding cries for help. I listened to it closely and followed it to the source. I used a small article of clothing to filter the smoke from entering my nose and then followed a series of burning and unsteady wooden stairs. The source of the cries led me to a room, engulfed in flame. I called out for the child, but received no reply. I then kicked down the burning door, fearing the worst. In front of me was an unconscious child, no mother; Just a child.

There had been cases where my intervention would mildly change the sequence of events established in my visions. This depended, in part, on the time of my arrival. Perhaps I arrived before the child and mother could be united. Maybe when I crashed into the building I damaged more than the window. I may have caused a pillar of the fragile building to collapse, blocking of the mother's path to the child. My unearthly dash to this location may have alarmed someone, who then thought to pursue me and intervene. The broken window may have fed the flames in a pattern that was inconsistent to the vision. I may have even opened a new escape route. There were many different factors to consider.

All I know is that this child is dying. I have to make my own decision like Shadow always suggests I should. Do I rescue this dying child or keep him here to look for his mother? There was nobody to make this decision for me. I'm incapable of making my own decisions. The child was dying with every second I spent pondering. The choice I make today may haunt me for the rest of my life. It was this day that I made my very own decision.

I held the helpless child in my hand and walked out of the dragon's mouth.

While we were outside I could hear the sirens from the approaching fire trucks. I placed the child on the ground and looked around for the mother. There was nothing. I nervously shook the child and fanned his smoke covered face in an attempt to bring him back to life. He slowly opened his eyes.

"Where is your mother", I frantically demanded.

The child raised his hand and pointed back towards the burning building. I turned my neck and was pierced by a scorching explosion. The building became more unsteady. I doubt it can hold its form much longer. In a few minutes it would all come crashing down.

Damn it! She was still in the building!

I looked around for the fire fighters, but they were not quite here yet. I made the wrong choice. I always make the wrong choices. I should have looked for her, she couldn't have been too far away from her child! If this child's mother died, then he would live the rest of his life just like I do.

The city was in a dire state of emergency. It felt as if everyone turned to me for help, they were all depending on me! I couldn't stomach the thought of letting this child's mother die. I didn't want to live with that on my conscience. I didn't want to add another mark on my wall.

I looked into the child's eyes; misfortune had forced tears down his rosy cheeks. I listened to the sound he made when he cried… until it became unbearable. He kept his eyes clasped to the building, hoping for a miracle. In his eyes I saw flames. More explosions occurred from within the building, and the fire fighters were still not here. So many thoughts ran through my mind.

I rose to my feet and charged back into the dragon's mouth.

"It's still not too late to correct my mistakes", I thought. "I won't let him down!"

I fought through the flames and worked my way towards the place where I had discovered the child. I called repeatedly, to get the mother's attention, but no one replied. The smoke was overwhelming, but despite it all, I continued to search thru each room fruitlessly. I was torn down to my last thread of hope. Thoughts of rescuing this woman from imminent doom seemed impossible. I approached the final room. It was entirely covered with a coat of smoke. I intruded into the final room; there was a figure beneath a fallen pile of wooden restrains. It was a woman. I quickly tore the heavy objects from further harming her delicate body. I cradled her in my arms; I was unsure whether she was dead or alive. The building was falling apart like ice sculptures to flame, and more poisonous smoke flooded our seldom air. The very floor beneath my feet was crumbling, stair cases had long been devoured by the hungry flames. There was no way down, I was trapped.

I desperately searched for another stair case and hoped that it was made of a flame resistant material. My search led me down the corridor to an emergency evacuation route. I was shocked to find a man standing in front of the exit. He wasn't alarmed by the burning building; no, he seemed to admire the destruction.

"What are you doing? You gotta get out of here", I shouted.

He paid me no mind.

I somehow knew that this man was responsible for the fire. He was standing in front of the exit, the only way out was thru him. The situation only worsened. The poisonous smoke began to take its toll. Everything around me was tumbling down. I took a step further—with the dying woman in my arms, and got a better look at the man who had caused all of this.

It was my father.

He turned only his neck to look at me; his feet remained firm. In his eyes I saw hate and emptiness.

"Don't you recognize me Papa", I began.

"I'm your little boy."

He suddenly lashed out his hand and slammed me against the wall.

He wrapped his hand around my neck and began to slowly squeeze the life out of me. My grip on the woman loosened, and she fell to the ground. Now with both hands free, I resisted him so frantically. He jabbed me in the face, and the back of my head crashed into the wall. I fell to the ground instantly. I was sure he would finish me off now, but he surprised me by showing me his back and slowly walking away. I guess he wanted me alive for a bit longer. My strength was drained. I was laying on the ground dizzy and light headed, while the hungry flames grew nearer.

With the last breath of my lingering soul I raised my voice to say, so angrily, "I didn't kill your wife father!"

"Mom willingly gave her only life to save my own! I want her back just as bad as you do! If I could rewind the hands of time then I would have took that bullet in her place. She is the one who truly disserved to live, not me. I should have died that day, not mama."

I was crying again.

I looked down at the child's mother who laid motionless directly beside me. In her I found the strength to continue on. I lifted her up and clumsily tried to free her from the burning home.

My vision became impaired. Every agonizing step I took led me further into imminent doom. My body could not meet this physical demand. I fell to my knees against my will and closed my eyes. Everything turned black.

"I'm so sick of it all", I thought to myself.

"I'm glad to go."

Chapter Four

Unwelcomed guest

Much to my surprise, I found myself nursed to good health. I questioned if the undesired thoughts, or the events which had be fallen me were simply that of a dream. My wondering eyes soon came across the ones who awakened me, perhaps the ones who rescued me. They were three individuals, who names and forms were blatantly unknown. One of the men wore jeans and a leather jacket. He was skinny with short blond hair neatly brushed backwards. The other man was well presented in a white tuxedo. He had brown hair, tanned skin and looked to be in his mid thirties. The last man was an old scientist. I say this simply because he wore the traditional white lab coat.

"My name is Johnny", said the man in the tuxedo.

"My name is Dr. Osco", said the old scientist.

"The gentleman next to me is Vince."

"Thank you for rescuing me", I said.

They all looked at each other, puzzled.

"We did not rescue you", said Osco. "When we found you you were lying unconscious in front of the burning building just past harm's length."

I was remorseful. I thought of the child that I let down. I thought of my own mother who gave her life to save my own. I considered my father's thoughts on having his precious wife taken away in my place. I felt as if I had destroyed something truly worth living.

"Who was she", questioned Johnny.

I looked to him in confusion and he made an effort to clarify things.

"There was a woman who laid beside you, we left her and her son to the care of the fire fighters."

I couldn't help but to smile. We had made it out… somehow.

"We also found this guy by you while the mother and child were gone", said Johnny.

Zeke bursted through the door and jumped on my bed! I was happy. I loved Zeke so much, he always stuck by my side and never let me down when I needed him most.

Johnny gave me an offered to live with him; I accepted. He was rich, had a very nice home, hell it sure beat living on the streets. I indulged in the finer things in life. I later discovered that, the three individuals, were close friends with my father, and were also part of the Oddity. The three individuals were good people, in them I found everything that I prayed to god for. They were even kind enough to enrolled me in school; however, I hadn't had much of an education since my mother died. I was doing poorly in school, I couldn't live up to the expectations that the three individuals made for me. I was letting them down and in time we began to grow distant. My heart and mind simply decided to run from it all. So one night Zeke and I escaped back to our secret construct. When I was in school, I remember falling in love with a beautiful woman named Nyru. The sweet memories I had of her remained with me till this very day.

In the night, I laid on the cold street, chained with the proceeding though of regret. I gazed at the ascending markings on the wall until it pained me to look. On this day the heavens too wept. There was no place I could call home, no place I could find refuge from the rain; and the thought alone made me sad… even sleep did not bring relief. It was then that I felt the gentle touch of a stranger, with that came the rain's impediment. I turned around, and to my surprise, found the image that dwelled in my reoccurring dreams. My electric eyes became hypnotized by her beauty. Her black hair expanded to the lowest part of her shoulder; rain trickled down her caramel skin and ran down her breast. The flow of the rain let her shirt drenched--- almost transparent. I looked away quickly in fear that she would think rudely of me. Our eyes met when I looked up. Her pearly black eyes filled with joy. We both stood under the same umbrella. Her lips were red like sweet Clementine, that in which I longed to taste. My lips dared not touch her own; however, in the merriment of my dreams, my lips had touched her a thousand times.

"Nyru", I said softly.

"It's good to see you again; though I had hoped that it would be under different circumstances."

"I've seen you here before", she began.

"I see you from a distance in this alley, talking to someone... I hear, but distinctively. Many times I cast away the thought of it being you who was alone in this dark alley, but since you stopped coming to school... I knew that it just had to be you. Why did you stop coming to school?"

"I was underachieving", I began.

"I tried and tried but despite my best efforts I would always end up failing."

"So you just decided to give up", she interjected.

"Look, nothing good ever comes to those who just sit and wait. I'm sure all you truly needed was tutors and some friends and I know you would have been just fine."

She examined my dirty wet clothes, un-groomed hair and withering shoes then asked, "Where are your parents?"

She found the answer within my silence and offered me to spend the night at her house. As we walked towards her home, she went on to explain that her older brother traveled away to college and that his room was made vacant. She spoke of what her eyes had seen and shared with me her interpretation of it. I smiled like some love struck fool; to me she sang like an exotic bird and I was grateful to be the branch in which she lay. We both walked further down the street under the same umbrella. Shoulder to shoulder, step by step. The rain falling on the umbrella was like music to my ears now. This was a truly romantic scenario, like living inside a wonderfully painted picture. I wished that this moment would never come to an end. I marveled at her beauty until my heart overflowed. I was truly happy, my heart and mind were without even a whisper of doubt.

We came across an apartment, worked our way up the stairs, and then she said "welcome home."

As I opened the door I was immediately greeted by the enticing allure of a home cooked meal.

"Nyru Naomi Krashew", began an angry woman.

"Why is it that a simple task like, getting ingredients for me from the grocery store, take u ages to complete? Your lateness has forced me to reconsider--"

She paused and focused her attention on me.

"Now who is this handsome young boy?"

My eyes became like that of an infant. I watched this woman so intently. Studying and making a mental image of her like a child would. This woman had a dark skin complexion and long hair as black as ink. She resembled my mother.

"His name is Chase Vega", said Nyru. She realized that I was taking much too long to answer such a simple question.

"Well Chase its very nice to meet you", said the mother of Nyru.

But I kept silent so all we shared was a smile of greetings.

"I have to fix up an extra plate for dinner. I wish you guys would tell me these kinds of things ahead of time. You should go and take a shower while I prepare dinner. I'll even have Nyru bring some worm clothes for you to wear."

The woman who embodied my dreams directed me to the bathroom and she left as I walked in. I stripped away my dirty clothes, and then stepped into the bath tub. The shower cleansed me, releasing what looked like mud from my body. I unwillingly climbed out of the shower, feeling fresh and anew. Nyru slowly opened the door. She used one hand to holding the clothes for me to wear and the other hand was shielding her eyes from my naked body.

"I brought these for you", she said in a voice soft spoken.

I delivered my thanks and then began to dress myself in her company.

"Dinner is ready," she said to me.

We both raced down stairs and took a seat in the dining table while her mother fixed us a hot plate. There was a man who I assumed to be Nyru's father. This man harbored dark black hair which neighbored a progressing bold spot at the top of his head. He didn't appear to be the tallest man. But what made me very uneasy about him were his eyes. He looked into my very soul, so intently that it became unbearable.

"Okay eat up guys", said Nyru's mother, braking the awkward silence.

I quickly dug my face into the food. Finishing it before the others could even get started. I went days without food.

"May I have some more", I begged.

This statement alone attracted the attention of others.

"Why... yes... yes of course", said the mother.

She then put another plate in front of me. The second was finished just as quickly as the first.

"May I have another", I said again.

"I'm afraid that was the last. I only prepared a meal to feed my family.

The displeased look on her face and the statement which followed both presented me with a problem. She was thinking of me the whole time, I was too zealous to realize that it was her plate she handed me. I felt that the best thing I could do was to stay behind and help with the dishes.

I remained when the others finished eating. I began to rack up the dishes when something very strange happened. Nyru's mother looked at me, turned away then looked at me again, but this time she wore my mother's face.

"I've been waiting for you to find me", said my mother in a tone which I found... agreeable.

"Mother, is it really you", I said in disbelief. But an answer was substituted by a song. She began to hum to me the song of emotions. I was so thrilled to see her again. I knew that she was the only one who could bring the erasure of anxiety. I hugged her tightly never wanting to let go.

"Mama, mama", I said triumphantly. "They told me that you were dead but I knew it was a lie. I missed you so much mama. Where did you go? That doesn't matter; just promise me that you'll never leave my side!"

"I'm not your mother", she began "So please don't call me that!"

I loosened my grip then realized that the face of my mother was no more. It was all just an illusion.

The unfamiliar room along with shifting dreams of darkness forced me to reclassify this as a sleepless night. I couldn't stop thinking about my mother, the pain that I must have caused Nyru's mother and her father's intimidating glare.

At times like these I search for a relief, something tangible, a substitute for ambiguity. And the first thing which crossed my mind was Nyru. She always made me happy, so I thought that if I saw her again then I would recall the happy moments that we shared.

I snuck out of my room late at night and found myself waiting in front of her door. Taking careful note of time, and then… slowly opened the door and intruded into her bedroom. Her half naked body lay tranquil on the bed in a manner I found… tantalizingly promiscuous. She wore covering for her chest, the bed sheets were thrown to the ground, and her legs… invitingly flung wide open. My heart began to race and… I could feel myself getting aroused.

I willingly grew closer to her; until the distance between us could be measured by inches. She inhaled softly, perceiving the illusion of a growing bosom. My hungry eyes led me towards her luscious thighs. I timidly stretched forward my hand and stroked her yearning flesh. The gloves prevented us from making direct contact. I then retreated that hand and used it to unravel myself as I climbed on top of her and merged our bodies to one. She immediately woke up, startled and confused at what her eyes were forced to witness. Her body rocked back and forth, like a fast moving pendulum. I used my hand to cover her mouth, which in return, disabled her from screaming. She began to punch me several times, but sadly, her hits grew weaker as she fell a victim to the venom of my eager thrust.

When I was all done, I came to realize what a horrible crime I had committed. I forged rivers of sorrow to pearly black eyes unused to flow. I released her and she cried for help soon after. But I had used her bedroom window as a route for escape. By the time her parents came to her rescue, I had already faded into the dark night. I had become a shroud in the shadows.

Chapter Five

I want you to hate me

I'm disgusted by myself.

I know you probably hate me now, Shadow. You've always been watching me, judging my every move. No darkness could escape your unearthly glare, so, for you to witness such a crime--- with naked eyes should serve as irrefutable evidence to spark wrongly suppressed hate. I betrayed the trust she placed in me. I am falsely, manipulative. I am that which is not perceived as myself. So, Shadow, kind friend, grant me this selfish request. Please hate me. Hate me for all eternity. Hate me as if I had destroyed all in which you cherished most in this world. Since I only hurt the ones I love, your safety will then be guaranteed.

"Those are fitting words", he began.

"But I refuse to hate you, even though you will me to. This woman, Nyru, you claim to love her, yet you did something so selfish and irrevocable. You acted to fulfill sensual needs without considering the damage it would leave behind. I believe you did that to her simply because you are afraid of being loved. By doing something so revolting to her now you guarantee that she will never love or hurt you in the future. It's the self fulfilled prophecy. You keep pushing everyone away from you, always; it's much easier for you to play the victim and claim that the entire world hates you without justification.

What I desperately wish to know, more so because you cannot find the answer yourself is, Chase Vega, why do you continue searching for a woman that's dead? The answer is so simple. Haven't you thought of it yet? You felt that your mother was the only person who could truly love you. Nyru and the three individuals all loved you; you knew that, so you did something that would make them hate you. You're afraid of being loved because of the pain it may leave behind. The pain of you losing your mother; even through her death you still latch on so desperately. Your father loved your mother just as you did. Knowing so, you began to develop a solitary hatred for your own father, just as he did with you; cringing at the very sight of them in an intimate posture. "She loves him more", you would think from afar. You both blame each other for the loss of your only loved one. The concept of love is as infinite as time itself. In the burning hearts of those who desire freedom lays the copious pain of having it revoked. Just as in your heart lies the pain of having love ripped away---

In Mute City's dark mist roared an angry beast. One who's painful cry shattered the barriers of my soul.

"Zeke", I said to myself.

He's in trouble! I ran as fast as my feet would permit to its source, the alley in which we often dwelled. Little did I know that I was heading straight into a trap. Zeke now squirmed in front of me, injured! My heart rate increased and all sound faded. My wondering eyes led me to a brown faced man who was placed firmly at the top of the building. His black dreadlocked hair resembled wool, no, better yet, large drops of rain. His fist was folded, his eyes burned with the desire to fight.

"What do you want from me", I demanded.

He gently leaped off the building with his hands horizontal and his hair levitating as he descended. He looked into my eyes as his feet reached the ground.

"My name is Kyle Bison", he began.

"I am the mighty Kyle Bison of the wind tunnel. I'm the strongest member of the new Oddity and have made it my personal role to cleanse this city and put an end to those who abuse their power; you are the last surviving member of the Zodant worrier tribe and have proved to be the strongest of the Oddities. "Is Chase stronger than Kyle?" This question has always troubled me. This battle will determine whose strength comes second only to Felix Crown's, and sadly bring the extinction of the Zodant Clan."

Rumors have integrated my father's achievements with that of my own. I, unlike my father, have never gotten into any major battle and the ones that I've won have been because of pure luck. So, chances are, I'm not a fraction of the opponent he expects. My heart raced as he grew nearer.

"This is what I've wanted right", I questioned myself.

Death for my sins; the angels in heaven would surly think poorly of me if I thought to take my own life in order to be reunited with mother. I should thank this murderer for doing that which I could not. Ending my life could be the best course of action for the entire world. But still I wonder, what of the happiness that this world once brought me?

My enemy grew dangerously near.

I fear that my future is entitled to nothing, my thirst for pleasure is always deemed zealous and punctually denounced by society. I have to take care of myself now. There's no one looking out for me. My persisting life exists so that I can retreat to the subtle pleasant times safely locked away in my ambiguous mind.

I glanced over at Zeke's helpless body; and so I can protect the ones I love.

My murderer now looked me face to face. Courage enabled me to break apart those lips once clasped by fear, and say to him, I wish to continue living!

His eagerness to fight compelled him to throw the first blow, just as I had expected. I avoided it and returned my own punch, that of a slightly greater caliber. He began hurtling a borage of punches, each doing massive damage. After stumbling to my knees I noticed myself slipping into a state of suppressed pain and adrenaline surge. It could best be described as being aware that you're dreaming, so much so that you could alter the course of the dream and predict what to come. My enemy's punches now seemed predictable, or slower. I was elusive and could land a punch on him with ease. In time, he realized that it was pointless, so he leaped back and tried a more devastating tactic. He threw both hands in the air then slammed them down to the ground. The earth shook beneath me and on the very dirt where my feet lay, emerged a bolt of lightning. My body became paralyzed. As the electricity came to contact and slithered its way towards the sky.

"What have you done to me", I shouted frantically.

But there was no answer. He propelled himself towards me and sent a borage of punches, some to my body but most aimed for my head. Each savage blow dented my body while I, however, was still left immobilized.

The paralysis finally wore off at too dear a time. I distend myself from him until I found the space between us agreeable. Kyle threw his hands in the air, slamming it to the ground and the electric serpent emerged from underneath my feet. My enemy tackled me to the ground and while he was on top of me, he bashed my skull into the cold pavement. I became light headed and slowly subdued to the pain. I pushed him off me, using the remains of my fleeing energy. I noticed that the ground where my head laid was red. I touched the area of my head where the pain was greatest. This blood was my own! I was plunged into a state of bitter hatred. I could hear his footsteps growing dreadfully near.

"Stay away", I demanded.

I then shut my eyes, giving in to the final blow.

I found myself in my abandoned home, in the very room that I slept. The room was lit poorly by a single candle. Its lingering light struggled to show me something. As I looked closer, I saw a figure on my bed. I approached with extreme caution. I stood at the foot of my bed, and then stretched forward my hand to remove the bed spread which had masked this mysterious figure.

"Dear god, this cannot be", I thought to myself.

What I saw on that bed was… myself. My head turned towards me, watching me with eyes ripped open by fear.

I woke up from my nightmare. My head was on the hard pavement. My face felt as if someone was wiping me with a wet towel. I looked to find the cause and was grateful to see my good pale Zeke in perfect health. I then began to examine my body, questioning how much was of a dream.

My shadow took shape, as he had done so many times before, but never had I been so reluctant to see him. He confirmed that last night's events were real and that Kyle Bison was not of my imagination. I steered the conversation and then began to ask him about my nightmare. The only comment he made before he faded away was that; a dream where one sees themselves, or becomes aware of two selves, is a strong representation of a near death.

I was troubled by his words. I knew that Shadow was of my image, therefore; I was aware of two selves.

I couldn't help but to wonder what happened to my opponent. A one-on-one fight to the death, never results in two survivors. My existence was clear, however, my acute memory lose and the lack of bodily evidence wouldn't allow me to overrule this case. Perhaps I ran from a losing battle, or maybe he showed me mercy. I rose to my feet and slowly began to realize how naive I've been. I came to this city many years ago in emboldened wishes of finding my mother. Yet I've accomplished nothing. I remembered what grandpa told me so long ago; if ever you should become lost, simply return to the place of origin and things would become much clearer. I was lost in a sense. I had to return to my place of origin. I had to go back to the place I had run away from ten years ago because I knew that beneath those walls was something that would tell me what to do with my life. I rose to my feet, and Zeke did the same; now with no reason to stay, we both decided to go home.

There was a construction site near the city limits and I paid no mind to it at first but Zeke was extremely hostile.

"What's the matter buddy", I questioned.

He ran towards a large down slop, which led to the construction site. And in that construction site was about a dozen lizard men. They had thick heavy tales, piercing claws, razor sharp teeth and their rough scaly skin was the color red and black. They were obviously venomous; and had swarmed around a common enemy like vultures moving in to kill a lingering prey. I grabbed Zeke and tried to tug him away from a battle that did not concern us. I took another look at the battle scene and realized that the lingering prey was the same kid from last night; Kyle Bison. Many thoughts ran through my mind, "should I help him?"

"Did he spare my life? Did he run from a losing battle? Is he a friend or foe?"

I spent much time debating on which course of action I should take. In time, the answer became so obvious.

"C'mon Zeke", I said.

"Let's leave him here."

I took one step away from the battle field and then realized that Kyle had seen me. I stood, as an observer, on top of a down slop. The sun had projected a giant shadow of me over the battlefield. This made it harder for me to simply walk away because now Kyle knew that I was here to make a difference. He looked at me; he was counting on me to save his only life.

It was then that a vision came to me. In five minutes Kyle Bison would die.

The Lord said that, "he who shuts his ears to the cries of another will someday cry and not be herd."

So with the lord watching, I went down the rocky slop to save his only life.

Zeke and I battled the scavengers with less than five minutes of Kyle's life withering away, like a delicate flower left too long in the heat. Our enemies began to retreat, which was fortunate because I had doubts that the time given would be sufficient. I got closer to Kyle and checked his pulse; he was still alive, surprisingly. His body seemed dismantled;

the time was ticking in the grim reapers favor. The hour glass was almost out of sand; his life was coming to a rapid conclusion. I had to make another decision, so I closed my eyes, touched his body and stole every ounce of pain he endured. My body bruised and bled, as his regenerated. All I felt was pain; my body was at its most vulnerable state. Kyle was awakening from him slumber. The results would be devastating if my enemy awoke so I used the last of my energy to lay on Zeke's back as we retreated to our place of origin.

Chapter Six

The perfect Lie

We lived at the top of a mountain which cradled such a wonderful view. Our home was hidden in the leaves; slowly we climbed to the top, growing closer and closer to the home that I swore never to return to. Slowly… slowly we climbed out of what felt like a desolate pit of misguided hope.

I arrived home to discover that the pulsating love that once strived in my home had too fled; never to return. The healing tree which grew in front of our home was no longer bright and radiant but rather dead and still. The leaves were an unavailing gray which crumbled to the very touch. Loathsome parasites had ravaged my once sweet home. The wooden frame of my home was putrid; it had blackened and become undone. My mother's grave was buried right next to my abandoned home. My heart too had become undone. I wept and cursed the decision I'd made. A dark cloud hung above me.

Then suddenly, much to my surprise, the world around me slowly returned to its former state. Everything began to heal itself. Flowers sprouted from the ash like impatient winter snow. My home returned a rich golden brown texture, hugged gently by blooming vines of velvet and pink. The sun kissed my face and persuaded a smile. I kept calm…

and admired this miracle. My eyes swung back and forth concurred by overwhelming curiosity.

Afterwards I realized that the tomb was no more. The enticing allure of food filled the air. There was a figure inside my home. I could no longer keep calm. My reactions were electric, visceral; I ran as fast as my legs would permit...

"What will happen next", I wondered.

I swung open my door and worked my way from the vacant living room to the kitchen. There I found a woman dressed in a beautiful velvet dress. She was preparing a stew and had not yet noticed me. I was tussled in a daze. I recalled the time when I mistook Nyru's mother to be my own, but this time was different. This time I was certain.

"Mama", I said soft spoken.

She turned her neck slowly towards me, looked into my eyes with a smile and open arms then whispered, "Hello Darling."

I innately dashed to her embrace, holding her dear in my arms. Her warm flesh brushed against my cheeks and comforted me. I closed my eyes and gave a sigh of relief, "my journey had finally come to an end", I thought.

I felt safe again, for the first time in years I felt love. I listened carefully to the song of her beating heart. I've found what I've been searching all these years for; I've found what I prayed to god for. She was the triumph of my heart, the vessel of my soul.

"Your eyes", my mother began.

"They look like you've been crying."

"I weep in time spent apart", I said with a smile.

"I wouldn't mind spending the remainder of my years in your arms; no, I wouldn't mind that at all."

"You remind me of a curious novel", she began.

"It was about a man who only found happiness in his dreams. He then, naturally, substituted the painful reality for the soothing contents of a dream. His entire life-- he lived a world of fantasy, a world in which he solely existed; nothing but self indulgence mattered."

"Is that wrong", I interrupted.

"It was a perfect lie", she began.

"His bias truth was equivalent to the reality of others. His clinical condition began as self fulfilled prophesies then frequently occurring delusions. In time, he came to realize that he was not dreaming, only then did he wake up from his dream. When he was cured he quoted to psychologists that "he felt as if he was trapped in an ambiguous world without the ability to dream."

"I don't mean to be rude but what does this have to do with me", I questioned.

She remained in silence, searching for the words best suited to express her deepest thoughts.

"The doctor recommended that book to me", she confessed.

"It was similar to your condition. You strive on self indulgence. You instinctively repress that which brings you pain, it's a beautiful act, I know; but by doing so you fabricate irrational delusions that will never truly come to pass. You ran away from home at such a tender age and returned lecturing on and on about an oracle, an imaginary pet named Zeke, and something called the Oddity. I knew that this was no longer child's play and that your delusions had become more sever. Soon after, you began telling me that your shadow could speak to you. What came next was most disturbing; you strongly believed that I had been murdered, even though I stood right beside you the whole time.

You ran away from home and never returned; that is, until now. I searched desperately for you Darling. Ten cold years have gone by since we last met, in time I found myself at a less of fate. However, the fact that you have returned implies that the medicine is working."

"Is all this true", I wondered.

I studied my own hands only to discover that leader-one's gloves did not exist. My hands were pure again. This could be true, perhaps the Oddity never existed. I reached out and touched the softness and warmth of my mother's face. I smiled a great big smile; it felt nice to feel again. All that had caused me harm was of my own doing.

Afterwards I wondered about Zeke. He could not have been entirely of my imagination. I longed to see him again. He never let me down. He was the only one who loved me unconditionally and he took good care of me as well. Impressions of him were engraved in my memory. I wish I was strong enough to live without him but I just can't do that. That would be asking too much of me. The thought alone made my heart sink a hundred thousand depths. I called for his name but there was no reply.

"Mama where is Zeke", I questioned.

"Zeke never existed", she began.

I restrained my urge to cry.

"I don't believe my eyes", I began.

"I trust my heart! My heart tells me that Zeke was real and that my feelings for him are true. I care about Zeke. Love is the strongest word I know and I truly love him Mama. He carried my joy for all these years... and shared my pain."

"The medicine must be wearing off," she interrupted; and then proudly reveled a needle, containing a solution, red like blood.

"Memories of him will be the last pain you ever feel", she said while inching the needle ever closer to my body.

"Should I believe only that which is seen", I questioned.

"Or perhaps that in which my heart's eyes defines as actuality? The civil war of my mind and heart waged on; leaving me with a dilemma. If I accepted the medicine—if I accepted the cure, then Zeke's existence would truly perish. If I denied the offer then my own mother would die. I clenched my fist and battled my thoughts for the reasonable solution. She bared the sum of my ambitions. My entire life was spent searching for her and that god-given love in which only she wielded.

I unclenched my fist, stretched forth my hand, and said goodbye to Zeke.

I shut my eyes to the discomfort to come. It was then that I heard the sound of the precious cure falling to the ground and shattering on impact. My mother had clumsily dropped it. I opened my eyes only to witness pain within Mother's changing face; then, caught her before she plunged into the kitchen floor.

"Are you alright", I questioned.

I cradled her weary body and was shocked to find my own hands stained with blood.

Her blood!

I turned around and to my surprise, found the same petulant kid from the night before, Kyle Bison. In his hands was a bloody dagger.

I struck his face with the sum of my hate and he fell to the ground, hard.

"That's not your mother", he struggled to explain.

"He is an illusionist; he's the Panoptic Bruiser! He tried to kill you just now!"

My mother called forth my name with a cold whisper, "Chase, Chase darling."

I rushed closer to hear her diminutive cry.

"I gave you all that you wished for", she began.

"You could have lived a perfect lie as well."

I looked to the ground just to find that the cure mother suggested was simply a lethal poison that seeped a gaping hole through the wooden floor. The Bruiser's illusion began to differ. Everything around me returned the way it once was. Loathsome parasites filled my kitchen floor, the walls of my sweet home were the color of death, and the trees too were dead and still. I looked at my hands to find that the glove which plagued me had returned. I wanted to touch her face and steel every ounce of her pain. Just as I had done time and time before. But Kyle wouldn't allow it. He pulled me back and was unquestionably successful in preventing initial contact between her and myself.

"Let me take the pain in her place", I demanded.

"Let me bring her back to life!"

But my words proved to be received in deaf ears.

My mother, I mean, the Panoptic Bruiser struggled to speak his final dying words.

"Do you know what happens at the end of that curious novel", questioned the Bruiser.

"The main character walks to the end of the earth. He jumps off the cliff with a smile, eager to hear the sound of his body crashing into the sharp rocks. In his dying thoughts, he wondered how the angels in heaven would look upon him for destroying his own life."

Those final words concluded the Bruiser's life. After the carnage—after the destruction had seized—when my eyes could weep no more, I still wondered in solitude… perhaps death was the only cure. The only absolute freedom there ever was. I was on my knees sobbing. My heart burned with the overwhelming pain of loss. Kyle stood watching me at my weakest state, without a word of comfort to spare.

The trees and grass bowed their backs to the presence of a landing plane. I assumed that it was Kyle's rid back to Mute City. I recognized the driver to be Johnny Sage. Sage looked into my eyes with a sense of disappointment. He didn't express words of sympathy or greetings.

Kyle turned his back to me and headed towards the plane. I was alone again.

"Do you think it's odd to pursue that which brings you absolute joy", I questioned the man who took what I valued most away from me.

"If my entire life was spent searching for love, would you think it was a life well wasted?"

He entered the plane with all my questions left unanswered.

"Are other people kind to you", he questioned.

I hung my head in shame and then said, "Zeke, he is kind to me."

"She", interrupted Kyle.

"Zeke is a female. You unconsciously refuse to accept love from any man. You believe all men are like your father. The concept of love can come from infinite sources. It's difficult to define the complexity of human relations. It's similar to differentiating what is truly right and wrong. You and your mother are of separate worlds now. You and your mother cannot co-exist. Some of the finest things in life cannot truly co-exist, like ice and warmth. This I have observed to be true. Have you ever really tried to love another?

I looked the ground face to face.

"Why did you come here", I asked.

"I have no ties to you, so why did you save my life back there?"

"I recall that you saved my only life", he said with a smile.

"Allowing you to perish would betray my morals."

My ears had never heard those words before, so I asked him, "What are morals?"

He looked at me with a blank expression; searching for the words best to define it. And then he began, "a moral is a sacred promise, a law signed by the sincere blood of the heart and mind; something that you will never do. Do you have any morals?"

I thought about his question for a long time. I thought about something that I would never allow myself to do, a self made law that I would never disobey, yet nothing came to mind. In time, he found the answer in my silence then stumbled upon another question.

"What will you do now that everything is gone", he questioned.

"I don't know", I replied softly.

"The love my mother gave to me, I lost again. I have no where else to turn to."

Kyle shifted to the edge of his seat and then padded the vacant space, signaling me to sit beside him.

"It's a beautiful day", he began.

"Let's hang out."

I climbed in the plane and sat by his side. Zeke did the same. The grass and trees bowed a final far well as we floated to the sky and said goodbye to my last remnants.

"What is it that brings you joy", I asked.

He stood in silence then turned his neck towards the window and looked at the clouds, and then later replied, "Fighting."

"Fighting brings me joy."

Chapter Seven

My Opposite Hand

We took to the skies and the trees beneath us waved their final farewell. I too, with a dry face, said goodbye to the last subtle remnants of my past, burring them deep in my memories as they should have been from start. I finally came to realize that I had spent my entire life searching for someone that had passed away so long ago. My emotions had made a fool of me. Those reoccurring visions of my mother were just the heart's way of telling me how much I missed her. The pain of longing to be with her became so overwhelming that I wished I could just die from it all. Everything that I held dearest to my heart is truly gone now. I tried so hard to rebuild what death had relentlessly undone. My mind was imprisoned in absolute solitude.

I exhaled with such an exhausted sigh.

"Did god intend for life to be this hard", I wondered.

I held Zeke tightly as the aircraft landed on top of Johnny's mansion like a bird on a nest.

"The Bruiser is one hell of an illusionist", I thought.

He actually led me to believe that, Zeke, the friend that's been with me for as far back as I could remember, never even existed.

Kyle so eagerly climbed out of the air craft. He stretched his body and then signaled his hand for me to come near. I quietly accepted. I approached him and he un-shyly began to speak to me as if we were old friends.

"Hey Chase, you ever been to the electronic lounge", he questioned.

I responded by slowly shaking my head no.

"Uh man", he began energetically.

"You don't know what you've been missing. It's the biggest hangout in the entire city. They have great food, music and the newest games. Today is the release of their newest game called "Loveless." We could be the very first to play it! My friends are there now… waiting for me. Would you like to come along!? They allow pets so Zeke can come along too."

I flashed a smile of acceptance.

We raced along the busy streets, covering a distance of approximately two miles. We managed to make it to the electronic lounge five minutes before they even opened. There was a long line at the door. Apparently we were not the only ones who wanted to play this game early.

Rather than wait in line like everyone else, Kyle instead snuck his way towards the unpopulated back entrance of the store. I followed the one who invites me; with such questionable compliance. In solitude I thought not of his present action but rather his intention for doing so. Why did he illegally sneak to the back entrance? I know this is wrong, perhaps fruitless from the start; yet I allowed him to guide me to a place in which we were both forbidden to come.

Around the back entrance were the friends he mentioned to me earlier about. There were only two of them; one male, the other female; a problem child and a misfit.

"Took you long enough to get here", said the problem child.

He then turned his eyes and neck towards me. "We don't permit outsiders amongst our crew."

"Yeah, yeah I know," Kyle interrupted.

"Don't worry, he's cool. He even saved my life once."

They both developed electric eyes and looked at me in pure amazement.

"Wow this guy saved the mighty Kyle Bison," said the chuckling misfit.

"Well I must confess I did see something interesting in his eyes. He's different from the rest… not to mention easy on the eyes."

I smiled a great big smile and my cheeks turned red with embarrassment.

"And look at his hands", the problem child interrupted.

"He wears Leader-One's gloves! Say, tomorrows the big day; he'll be joining you right?"

The room grew with an uneasy silence.

"What did he mean by the big day", I thought to myself.

"What's going to happen tomorrow? His words left me in wonder, and Kyle freely took on an obligation to break the silence, "are we gunna hold hands and talk all day or are we gunna be the first to play Loveless?"

"Oh my god your right", said the problem.

"We've wasted so much time already, the store is about to open up.

He bent his arm and looked at his wrist watch with a dissatisfied expression.

"This is the plan! The entire electronic lounge arcade systems all run on an old fashion type BB6 anti pirating firewall. Shutting off the main power supply would reset the entire system. The system would then each need a manual reboot. The main power switch is located in the security room, fortunately for us the entire security staff members are at the entrance taming the heavy crowd who are wild and drunk with excitement. This plan is fool proof, however there is an uncalculated risk factor, if some dumbass informs an employee that the games are free of charge then we would all be busted.

"We can be the first ones to play and beat loveless", Kyle interrupted.

"Electronic lounge owes us something in retune after all the money we invested into it."

The entire group gave a silent smile in approval of the idea.

"This is our gift to you Kyle", said the misfit.

The problem child then interrupted to say, "yeah, a great gift for an even greater friend."

The tough guy: Kyle Bison, grew a secret smile on his chocolate face. He looked down upon his own feet and tried to whip away that unwanted smirk.

We rushed to the sealed door of the security room. They were blind to the word, "prohibited" and picked the lock with such miraculous speed. This was clearly not their first time. Their actions worried me. What we're doing is wrong. We were sure to get in trouble for this, we would be collectively hated criminals. I was frightened by uncertainty. I never thought that I would compromise with behavior such as this.

The problem child discovered the main power switch and slammed it down with little time to spare. Now the room was darker than night. I could hardly identify the hands in front of me.

A female voice was first to speak, "hold on guys I have a flashlight somewhere here", said the misfit.

She stumbled around in the darkness for some time and then triumphantly declared, "Eureka, I think I've found it!"

"That's not a flashlight your holding", said Kyle with a sexual connotation.

Kyle and the problem child burst into laughter, I laughed along with them too.

"That's not funny you guys", said the misfit.

"I really do have a flashlight in my hand, see."

The flashlight flickered like a firefly trapped in a jar, then died immediately. She shook the flashlight in hopes of restoring what little life was left in the dead battery. It became more of a humorous scenario the more she fought to justify her claim. We laughed so hard that we nearly cried from it.

The problem child turned the power back on and with a smile, demanded that we all enjoy the free video games, with that said, we raced to the first two arcade stations titled "Loveless". We merged with the crowd so security couldn't tell that we've been their the entire time. The game was two player co-operative play. The problem teamed up with the misfit, and I teamed up with Kyle. Together we fought through levels one...two...seven...eight, until we reached the final boss. Both our eyes were red from playing this game for so long. I turned my neck to see that the misfit's team was at a lower level. Kyle and I began the final battle with optimistic wishes and the sum of the knowledge and skill we inherited from the previous battles. The final boss began the fight by using a devastating move that depleted the remainder of Kyle's life. I was left alone with the arduous task of slaying the final boss. I gave it my all and lost so miserably. I released an exhausted sigh, and read the words "game over" written on the screen. I could see Kyle from the corner of my eye; he looked at me so intently. His action left me in discomfort; I turned my neck slowly until our eyes met.

"Relax", he said.

"You're trying too hard. Don't just rush in. first, study the pattern and the speed of his moves, and then plan your defense and counter attacks accordingly."

We tried again and again but the result remained the same.

The problem child then approached our arcade station with a frightened expression.

"Yo Kyle", he began.

"There onto us; we gotta get out of here!"

Kyle and I were discouraged from loosing and were about ready to call it quits. We quickly exited the electronic lounge as discreetly as humanly possible; with no time spent questioning the sincerity of the problem child's words.

The day aged to its weary years; we, before absolute nightfall, agreed to have dinner at a food stand nearby. They served cheap food, or what the trio referred to as, "a poor man's meal." We sat by Mute City's gutter and icy concrete down curve to enjoy our bland tasting meal. I brushed away most of the food off my plate and onto the floor for Zeke to eat. We shared embarrassing stories with each other, and laughed heavily, like drunken friends do. It came time to say goodbye; and all four of us rose to our feet and prepared to go our separate ways.

"Goodbye Kyle", said the misfit with weeping eyes. She then stretched out her hands and gave Kyle her final embrace.

"Come back to our crew; you understand?"

Kyle remained silent, his taught guy persona disabled him emotionally. He stretched out his hand to shake the hand of the problem child, like the traditional way in which two men greet and bid farewell. The problem child then brushed Kyle's hand to the side and hugged him, humanely—affectionately. The emotionless taught guy soon wrapped his arms around the problem child, and finally hugged him back, like a caring brother would.

I stood silenced by my own ignorance, as the trio showed each other their backs and went their separate ways.

"What's going to happen tomorrow", I wondered now more seriously than ever.

Shoulder to shoulder, Kyle and I walked back to Johnny's mansion, where we would spend the night. Again I tried to ask him about tomorrow, but just as I had mustered the strength to speak, he paused my breath to question, "Have you read the book called loveless?"

I shook my head no and he began to explain. That book took place in a planet called Earth. It was the year 2012 and they were evacuating uninfected humans into the Iron Bison. The ones exposed to that incurable virus would remain on Earth to die while the healthy came to this planet; Mute. Well anyway, there was a biracial couple, torn apart by the virus. "Why do you love that strange man", said the racist father in strong disapproval of his daughter's decision to die on earth with her husband. The daughter smiled through the chaos and said, "The opposite hand loves the other." She loved the man that could do what she could not, the opposite that complemented her own errors and imperfections. In comparison, you and I are two different hands; you are frightened by uncertainty, as you've clearly demonstrated. I, on the other hand, am drawn to the strange mystery that ambiguity brings. You're afraid to be loved...

He put his very words to a hush, in fear that he may strike at a fragile nerve.

I mean, by keeping others at a distant you elude the pain of loss. The irony of your actions is that mankind cannot live without the interactions of others. All human minds are at constant change, learning, evolving and adapting to different stimulus. Living is defined as the ability or willingness to embrace change. Other people's interpretations of your actions do not define who you truly are as an individual. You can't bear to be hated by the ones who you let down, so when things get too hard you just run away. You and I are truly different. It's fascinating; I think I may have been born just to meet you."

He ended his speech with a smile. I smiled too; Kyle became my first real friend! We arrived at Johnny's mansion and made our way to the room that we would spend the night. Kyle's bed was at the opposite end from my own. We slept in the same room, like brothers do, and finally I asked him, "What's going to happen tomorrow?"

He grew silent...

"Tomorrow is the day in which we were manufactured for", he replied then drifted to sleep.

I was on my bed lying awake for some time. My final thoughts of the night were of that damn video game. Despite our combined efforts, we simply could not beat the final boss.

Chapter Eight

The Final Boss

I awoke the following morning from a wonderful dream. In the dream I was a womanizer with a fleet of beautiful women who expressed a passionate moan in the nearness of my loving embrace. My poetic language made them all surrender their bodies to me. I turned my head to the opposite end of the room to find that Kyle was gone. His bed was neatly made, which seemed to be a bit out of his character.

"Kyle", I thought.

"Where have you disappeared to now?"

I rose to my feet and then went to the bathroom to groom myself.

"Today's the big day", I said to Zeke.

We worked our way downstairs and headed towards the kitchen. There was no one there, we were greeted by absolute silence. I found it difficult to recall the last time we had a filling meal; so I prepared breakfast using whatever I found laying around in the fridge. Zeke and I drank and ate together…alone. When we were thru, I washed up the plates and put the kitchen back as I saw it, like a good guest would.

Now that Kyle was gone—I mean, with no reason to stay—I had my last drink and decided to go, to where I did not know.

I gently opened the mansion's front door to discover dozens of elite solders armed and dressed in black military attire. There I found giant war vehicles cradling weapons of such fatal destruction. Amongst the army of men was a boy just like me!

"Kyle", I called out.

He acknowledged me and I began to make my way towards him. He was the only soldier unarmed; his hair was tied backwards, away from his face. He was on one knee, lacing up his dark green military boots. He was not quite dressed yet. His shirt was off and as he rose to his feet I could see that his body was covered with ugly scars! Burn marks, slashes, bullet wounds, thick scratches that people often gain from falling on hard ground; hell, anything you could think of was right there on his canvas. He was truly the product of war. This young boy's love for fighting was expressed so clearly now, however today would prove to be his final fight. You would not return with one or two scars to display like trophies; this time your thrilling adventure would not be painted on your body, but instead carved into your eternal tomb for loved ones to weep. My eyes grew unsettling. It pained me to look at his body this way, and Kyle knew it too; so he quickly masked his old wounds with a black shirt.

"I got those scars from the first time I fought Felix Crown", said Kyle.

"He let me live, he could have easily killed me right there and then but he let me live. My survival was not as an act of kindness I assure you; it was more of a long term investment. His intention was to raise me like cattle until I had grown big enough to satisfy his hunger for battle. I've spent so many years training for this rematch. I confess that fighting you was also part of my training."

All the men were ready and seated themselves firmly in each military vehicle. There heads were turned; waiting on the youngest soldier to enter.

The expression on Kyle's face was unyielding, I sensed that something was troubling him; he wanted to ask me something, I could feel it. He opened his mouth, however, to speak only words of parting…

"Goodbye Chase", he said with a smile.

He showed his back to me and headed into that war machine to sit with the other soldiers. He turned his neck towards me and said with a seldom breath, "the world will be a much better place once Felix is gone, I promise."

With that said, the vehicle's massive engine awakened; the engine made the same sound men make when they cry. The roar from the massive motor shook the walls of my chest. The vehicle drove further and further away from me. In solitude I thought, "What would I do now that my other hand is gone? I carried through my days without a purpose. Would I go back to living in that dark alley like some unwanted creature?! Or would I search another thousand years for my dead mother? I had to make another decision…

The vehicle drifted further from me. The narrow river that once separated our two bodies had now turned into a distant gulf. I was at a risk of losing my best friend forever.

I thought of the night before, and how he said that we were perfect opposites, he even went the extra mile and counted the ways in which we differed. But he left out one significant difference; I'm horrible at making my own decisions so my conditioned reflex for this internal dilemma is to beg for other's to help me and make decisions on my behalf. Kyle, on the other hand was much too stubborn to beg for help. He viewed it as a sign of weakness. That's what he's been trying to ask me all this time! He needed my help on this day. I ran as fast as I could towards the departing war machine. The vehicle had now gained a distance of about one hundred yards from me--One hundred yards and counting. I waved my hands frantically in hopes of attracting the curious attention of one of the soldiers. I yelled at the top of my voice, "Let me help you, let me help you Kyle."

It was too late. My words were heard in the soldier's deaf ears. They were all oblivious to my actions, all but one; the youngest soldier ordered the driver to stop. And the war machine came to a screeching halt. I neared the vehicle to arms length. I took time to catch my breath and looked Kyle in the face.

"Let me help you", I said.

"You can't do this without me!"

His face wore a very kind expression. Kyle offered me his hand and reeled me into the vehicle. I sat right beside him, Zeke entered the war machine immediately after me and laid in the center isle by my feet. I was content with the choices that I've made. The vehicle began its way again towards its final destination. We left Mute City and ventured into uncharted areas of the forest. The vehicle was with an unprecedented quietness. I knew remaining silent and not speaking unless you're spoken to was the first thing every soldier learns in basic training. But my mind couldn't help but to wonder of the piercing thoughts concealed in their solitary minds. They all looked empty inside, as if they were without a past. There was however one soldier who defied the orders of basic training and spoke out of term.

"Why don't you two have your guns", he said referring to Kyle and myself.

"We don't need them", Kyle replied.

"Uh I see", said the talkative soldier.

"You guys have the bloodline needed to use the power gloves."

He chuckled to himself and then held his gun close with trembling hands.

"I don't know what good that will do", he began.

"I heard that Felix can trap your mortal body in another dimension and torture your soul for a thousand years, just from looking into his yellow eyes. When he spits you back to the real world, friends will say that you have only been gone for three minutes. In just a few short minutes he can torture you for what will feel like an eternity. Some have even told me that if you should somehow manage to kill him, his evil spirit will haunt your once pleasant dreams and drive you to clam your own life."

The fearless Kyle Bison rudely blocked his ears with loud music. Now he too was deaf to this soldier's terrifying confession. I was the only one who offered listening ears; the talkative soldier knew this too. He reached into his wallet to show me pictures of his family.

"This is my beautiful wife", he began.

"I tell you, the way in which we met makes the content of a perfect love story."

He was smiling. I know he was recalling the day that they first met and the pleasant moments afterwards.

"That's my son next to my wife", he pointed out.

"He's got an amazing pitching arm. He can even go pro. I know he's only six years old but I read somewhere that when people develop an interest in something at a young age they end up mastering it in adulthood. Behind my family is my shiny new sports car. I purchased it before I enrolled in the military. I know it's an ill advised thing to so; hell, I've never been too good at managing money. Well I finished all the payments last month, now the car is officially mine! My wife called me to tell me the good news a couple days back. She also told me that she's expecting a baby girl—I couldn't control myself the last time we visited."

He paused and chuckled mischievously to himself. His face wore a happy expression. Today is April 4th, I was scheduled to be discharged by the end of the month. In just a couple of days I could have been home playing catch with my little boy and driving my shiny new sports car around town. Why if this suicide mission was postponed for just a couple more days I could have been living in paradise. I enrolled in the military to provide a better life for my family. I never really thought that I would die out here. I was a naïve and reckless teenager who truly believed that nothing life threatening could ever befall upon me, I guess those characteristics followed me to adulthood. Did you notice that I'm not in the picture with my wife and son? Of course you're probably thinking that it's because I'm the one who took the picture. That is true, but now I realize the true meaning why I'm not in this picture. Have you realized it yet? It's kinda ironic—the reason why I'm not in that picture is simply because God did not intend for me to have a future with my family. The stars and cosmos gave me a sign in this photo. I bargained my own life! For what, a shiny new sports car that I'm never gunna get to drive; and frankly could have done just fine without! I'm not a poor man; my family does not live their lives in moderation. I was as content as a flower before I enrolled in the military. It is the devil's greed that brings me to my trembling knees. Greed is what forsaken me. I'm a fool; I should have realized the secret message in the photo much sooner. It's too late now, were all going to die here! It was hopeless from the start. I know you all can hear me—the universal though fills all our minds. Nobody can live thru this; we're all going to die!"

His words scared nobody but me. If Felix was even a fraction of what these stories claimed him to be then we were all goners. The war machine inched us closer to our eminent doom. Our hand was being pulled nearer to the range of the deadliest snake.

"Stop the Vehicle", I demanded—hoping that the driver had not also grown deaf.

"We're running behind schedule as it is", said the driver.

"Please sir", I pleaded.

"Spare me just one moment of your time, there is something that I must do."

The vehicle came to a steady halt.

I used my god given judgment to cowardly assert myself from the war machine's grasp. The curse of silence was broken; all the soldiers mumbled silently about my actions. Kyle wouldn't even allow himself to look me in the face. He was disappointed in me.

The driver however, agreed to wait just one minute for me; one minute was all I needed. Yes, the talkative soldier's words frightened me, but my safety did not define my actions. It was the last member of my family that I was most concerned about, Zeke. I turned my back to my fellow soldiers and walked to a distance in which I found to be agreeable.

Zeke followed me, as if it were the only thing he knew.

"It was a beautiful day today", I said to Zeke.

"The weather resembled the time we first met. Do you remember that day?"

I paused to recall the time in the Oracle's home when he saved me from a poisonous snake.

"The road to our destiny has divided", I began.

"Our lives are parallel now. I can't guarantee your safety much longer. Where I am to go you may not follow."

I fell to my knees as if my legs lacked balance and gave Zeke my final embrace. I tightly wrapped my arms around him with a complete disregard for the time.

The driver honked the horn, signaling that my time was up.

I slowly loosened my grip and gave a solitary prayer for this moment to be eternal.

"You have to live amongst the wild now", I said.

"It was selfish and foolish of me to endanger your life for this long. There's no time anymore, goodbye old friend. I may never see you again Zeke."

Slowly I rose to my feet and turned my back to my childhood friend. As I was making my way back into the war machine, I could feel Zeke's presence proceeding. I turned my neck to discover him following me again. I pushed him away from me and he fell to the ground; he was happy, he thought that we were just playing one of our old games. He pranced back and forth playfully and energetically. I yelled and pointed for him to go afar. Although he could not understand my words; he interpreted clearly the seriousness of my facial expression. His playful behavior died instantly. Zeke took a step forward with every step I took back. I took a rock from the ground and threw it at him. The rock hit the sand near him and splashed sand like a wave into his face. Loathsome grains of sand entered his delicate eyes. Yet he still marched onward towards me.

I threw another stone! This one struck him on his front legs.

"You may not follow", I yelled so angrily.

The stone made an unpleasant thud sound as it crashed against his soft flesh. He gave a heart breaking yelp and without my comfort, tried desperately to suppress the pain. He was alone and bleeding. He limped towards me, slowly. I took another stone from the ground and sent it crashing into his flesh.

"Leave me alone", I demanded.

His face wore a melancholy expression, but he still marched toward me. I bent down to grab another stone, Zeke closed his eyes shut and bowed his head; awaiting the physical harm. I threw the stone, and it struck him in the back. He lifted his head and limped slowly towards me again. I picked up another stone. Zeke shut his eyes and bowed his head again, waiting to be stoned.

I dropped the stone to the ground and turned my back to my oldest friend. I could no longer bear to harm him. I re-entered the war machine leaving Zeke behind. The injured Zeke tried to enter the vehicle with me, limping every step. We drifted further and further away from him. He tried his best to keep up--He tried his best to reach me but his damaged legs did not muster the strength needed. I watched him nearly die from exhaustion, I watched him struggle desperately to be near me and I watched him disappear into the horizon. I fought back my urge to cry.

Nobody spoke a word in the war machine, including me. Now all the soldiers were truly deaf, as good soldiers should be. Another vision came to me… in ten minutes Felix Crown would destroy us all.

Chapter Nine

The final boss II: dreams of a mad man

We neared ourselves into harm's length, we were so close to death now; so close to Felix Crown that I swear I could hear him breathing. The war machine came to its final destination.

"We had entered devil's territory", I declared in solitude.

Just outside an eerie cave awaited the final two military convoys. We were obviously late. The soldiers began to exit the vehicle to reunite with the members of the other convoy. In time I found myself submerged in a sea of approximately forty military personals. I had never been amongst so many people before. I felt lost and out of place; I didn't like it, I didn't like it at all.

There was another person within this sea of people that struck familiar to me, Johnny Sage. He played the role of a military adviser; he was the commander of this operation.

"Alright ladies", he began.

"This is the moment we've all been training for. Today we free mankind from the shackles of the eternal overseer. Today we continue where the first Oddity soldiers left off. We cannot undo the physical and emotional scars this man has left in our present generation but we can allow our children to live in a world without his terrine."

All the soldiers cheered in support of his convincing speech. I wandered if the talkative soldier was also convinced by his speech. But unfortunately I had lost him already in this uniformed crowd.

"We are fortunate enough to be given leader-one's grace on this fateful day", he said pointing at me. All forty soldiers turned their necks towards me; they gave a loud roar of approval. They were placing the very fate of the entire world in the hands of a little boy.

"How foolish", I though.

Johnny Sage began to speak, "Alright ladies, standard bridge formation. Kyle and Chase will lead from the front. You will head to the southern part of the cave where Felix resides. I'll take just a handful of soldiers to the east where the original Reece Vega dwells. After the hostile has been destroyed my team will activate an NN1 bomb (near-nuclear prototype one bomb) that is set to explode in ten minutes. This weapon has the strength to take this entire infrastructure down and anything in it. Keep your heart beat monitors on! Let's do this quick and go home!"

"Yes sir", the soldiers replied simultaneously.

Johnny, with such a small squadron, disappeared into the caves dark mist; off to destroy my father's clone. My squadron went a separate way, southbound; towards Felix. We had a much greater man power, which presented the question, "does Felix Crown out power the original Reece Vega by this multitude?"

We ran deep into the eerie cave, and much like Johnny's squadron—we also were swallowed by the dark mist. Behind me was an army of elite soldiers and in front of me was Kyle Bison. The eager Kyle Bison out ran everyone and we feared that we would lose him in this darkness. It was as if Kyle had waited his entire life for this moment.

We were close to Felix now; I can hear him breathing so clearly now.

"You have inherited my bitter hatred", echoed the voice of Felix Crown.

We neither paused to curiosity nor halted from fear. We continued to move forward; unyieldingly. I silently asked myself; "how come Vince

Mansheeno didn't join us?" this is the most important fight. We could use any help we could get.

"It's human nature to defy the will of God and create a monster", Felix began.

"Just as it is a monster's instinct to destroy its creator. I destroyed the ones who corrupted me, the ones who made me into this monster! I killed my enemies.

We continued deeper into the darkness and could hear his frightening voice much clearer.

"You watched as they tortured me so long ago, all of you! Every breath was an insult to my name. For that you have inherited my bitter hatred; o, child of my enemy. Is it redemption which compels you to intrude into my sacred layer? If so I must warn you that my heart can offer no forgiveness; for those sins of your ancestors have transcended thru countless generations. Come closer and seal you fate. You cannot kill me! I made the grim reaper beg for my mercy before destroying him! Hell un-wants me. The ground shall quake if you burry me!"

We ran until we came to the end of the cave. It was a vacant room with nothing but a throne placed in the center of the room. Initially we thought it was a regular throne of metal, brass or ivory. However, upon closer observation we discovered a devastating truth. The throne was made from human bones and flesh. The room itself was intoxicated by a putrid stench, blood!

"Eternal life has taught me patience", Felix began.

"Like a god, I watched you two grow with such absolute patience, waiting for you to mature, waiting for you to reach your true potential. Yet you come foolishly at such a tender age. My hunger for war will not be denied. The day has come! Give me now a valiant battle! Destroy me! Destroy me! Come and show me what pain feels like!"

The walls of the cave trembled to his demonic voice. And right there, appearing as swiftly as lightening flashing before our very eyes was the immortal Felix Crown; the devil himself.

Kyle, unlike the elite soldiers, kept very calm in the face of danger. He turned towards me to reassure my decision.

"Are you frightened", he questioned.

"There's still time, you can still run away. I won't think anything bad of you."

"I won't run away", I said.

"I won't leave your side, our fates have intertwined. I'll stay by your side to <u>the</u> <u>bitter end</u>."

The soldiers all wore a frightened expression. Their trembling fingers clasped ever so closely to the trigger, waiting for just one false movement. The intimidating Felix Crown took just one step towards us; the forty soldiers, who were already at the verge of retaliation, fired their automatic rifles at a common enemy.

Felix reached out his hand and froze the bullets, just as they were about to pierce his flesh. The frightened soldiers kept their finger wrapped firmly around the trigger until their guns were all empty. We waited anxiously for the thick gun smoke to clear up. In front of him was an angry horde of bullets, distilled around his pale skin like a dark cloud.

"Everybody take cover", Kyle loudly demanded.

Suddenly, Felix waved an invisible wand and redirected the bullets back to the ones who dared to fire at him. Our allied troops fell to their knees as the horde of bullets penetrated each vital organ. Half of the elite soldiers we brought along for this mission had perished in a matter of seconds. The less fortunate ones did not die instantly. Instead they fell to the ground and struggled to breath, like a fish out of water.

"Stop this Felix", Kyle bravely demanded.

"You can't truly believe that what you've been doing to humans is right. Eternal life should bring you wisdom!"

"I gained all my wisdom while imprisoned in my mortal years", Felix replied.

"Eternal life has taught me patience alone! Can you, in your short life, claim to truly comprehend the ambiguous complexity of right and wrong?"

"As a child I understood the difference", Kyle interrupted.

"You're killing innocent people!"

"I'm simply destroying their bodies to set their soul free, I'm giving them an eternal piece of mind," said Felix.

"You were raised in pretence. Your predecessors have led you to believe incorrectly."

"That's no justification", Kyle yelled.

"In your life you've killed thousands of humans. What you're doing is homicide!

"What I'm doing is bringing world peace", Felix corrected.

"Is that not what you Oddities originally fought for? In a sense I'm just like you; right and wrong is all just a matter of perspective."

The protagonist and the antagonist engaged in a heated argument regarding the concept of right and wrong. I stood hidden in the shadows as they persecuted each other's actions and beliefs. In time I grew unsettling; and with courage, climbed out of the darkness to voice my own opinion.

Felix looked at me with those haunting yellow eyes. Very few people had the strength to stand up to him or even look him in the eye.

"The second key", he said referring to me.

"Chase India Vega, my how you've grown."

"My mother's dead", I said.

"I know that she's dead now. She meant the world to me. She was the last source of happiness I had and you took that away from me without hesitation. There are people in this world just like me; I've studied this to be true. In my short life I've seen people fall in and out of love, weep from the tragic pain of loss, and I've also seen those same people happy… and dancing. I've seen men on their knees crying and desperately praying to God for good fortune. My eyes have also seen romantic men on that same knee proposing to their wife to be. You wish to destroy this world and all the fine things it offers."

"Indeed", he began.

"My dream is to return it all to nothingness, to mold all minds into one without these unnecessary bodies. I will put an end to all emotions, doubt, pain, regret, sorrow; all these dramatic emotions will be of no meaning.

"This is death," I interrupted.

"You wish to bring fatal destruction upon the human race."

"Once again, that is just a matter of perspective", he restated.

"The new world is a white canvas. In this new world all minds and bodies will be merged into one single entity. All your darkest sins will be pardoned."

He generously reached out his hand towards me and gave me an offer that I found very difficult to refuse.

"Nyru would forgive you for what you've done," he began.

"You and I are the second and third keys. Together we can help make this dream a reality. This is the end of your life's journey; your mother patiently awaits you just outside these earthly gates. She's waited so long for you; don't you want to see her again?"

I would be a liar if I said that I did not consider his offer, but then I came to realize that this was the man who organized my Mother's death. I declined the devil's offer.

"My mother was the world to me", I said soft spoken.

"She put meaning into my life with such gentle hands. Now that she's gone, now that my life is of no meaning… I'll gladly risk it to defeat you. Your dream seems so heartless. Who are you to make a decision like that for the entire world? You're crossing into God's territory!"

He offered me his hand, which was filled with such tantalizing promises. When I denied his offer; he clenched that generous hand into a belligerent fist and gave me a devilish grin.

"Dear boy", he began.

"I am God!"

He swung his hand in an upward motion and generated a black ball the size of a moon. Everything that black moon touched seemed to erode and melt away. It left a path of destruction as it charged closer towards me.

I was frozen with fear. Kyle came to my rescue and tackled me out of harm's way. The black moon however, continued along that path of destruction and charged into the remainder of our allied troops. I turned around slowly and my eyes grew wide with terror; the black moon gathered them all to the seldom gates of their mortality. Their once young flesh seemed to age a thousand years. Their old arms lacked strength… and their weapons fell to the ground. These young men were all suddenly forced to their weary years. There was nothing I could do. I watched as the youth was dragged out of their bodies.

A man in the crowd struck familiar to me; it was the talkative soldier from before. He recognized me too; he recognized the only one who was willing to listen to the story of his beautiful wife and little boy. He clumsily walked to me with empty hands that seemed to beg for salvation. He grew closer and closer to me, aging a hundred years more with each dragging step he took forward. His young skin, once rich with color, now grew pale and unavailing. His skin was shriveling up, like some unwanted raisin. His boney hands looked like it would crumble to the touch. It was far too much to bear.

I closed my eyes.

I wished this man would just surrender. I wished him peace… I wished him death.

In time he lacked the will to survive and fell upon those brittle knees. His body continued to age, so much that it turned to dust, and was taken by the wind-- like the ash of a cigar.

I held this stranger's life with so much value. And in time, the thought of regret began to haunt me. The talkative soldier left one thing behind of unimaginable value. I took the picture of his family and safely tucked it in my back pocket in hopes that someday it would somehow navigate me to sooth his morning family.

I had my back facing the enemy, which was the biggest mistake anyone could make in battle.

I felt a soft touch on my shoulder; it was Kyle.

"Have you realized what today is", he asked that familiar question.

I raised my hand in frustration and swiped his hand from my shoulder.

"We have an onerous task presented before us", I said.

"Don't bother me with that repetitive question! You can't beat Felix Crown alone, the task is beyond you. You need me to help you fight; I'm not a fool Kyle. You've been meaning to ask me this favor since we were at the mansion but your pride wouldn't let you beg for help. I'm convinced that the only reason why you were ever nice to me—the only reason why you saved a seat for me and let me play that arcade game with you was just so you could gently persuade me to help you. I'm just some pathetic loser that you found from the street. You've realized the importance of my gloves and now you want to use me to guarantee your survival. All those kind words that you told me were just intricate strategies that would lead me to this exact moment. You need me here with you; I mean nothing to you otherwise. Your love for fighting may even be as false as our friendship."

"You think you've got me figured out but that's not it at all", said Kyle.

Just as he began to speak a warp gate opened up directly behind me. I turned to see if any danger would emerge from the shining light. Kyle did not pay the warp gate any mind, so then I thought that maybe he was the one who created it.

"I'm not like that Chase; I'm not like that at all. I don't have a mama or a papa. I was not born from a woman like most people, but instead created in the same manner in which you create deadly weapons and machinery. Felix Crown wanted someone who could give him an admirable fight. After he killed Donté the great and Leader-One there was nobody who could compare to his strength. That's when they started creating me. I was built for that purpose alone. I enjoy fighting because I was designed that way. Even my name is of paste.

The Iron Bison was co-developed by a company called Growth industries. Initially the company developed chemical compounds to help grow larger vegetables at an expeditious rate. Shortly after their success they created a second branch that used a similar compound but on humans; the second branch was called Kylee Tech. I'm sure that's where my name originates; Kyle Bison. I was sad when I heard the news because deep down I always pretended that one scientist found something special in me and took time when creating me. I believed I was something significant; I thought someone gave me an honorable name that would foretell the strong and brave man I would grow up to be. Now I've come to realize that the name that I've been answering to all these years consists of company logos that were carelessly scattered across the laboratory that bore me. So don't tell me what it's like to be used because I've been used my entire life I would never dream of treating you that way. What bothers me most about you is that you carry your life with little value. When good fortune comes your way you somehow find a way to diminish it. And look, you still haven't realized what today is! April 24th; today is the day that we planned the attack, yes. But more importantly today is your birthday. You're 19 years old today Chase.

I was completely against the idea of having you come to this wretched place; I was more than willing to do this alone. I belong in this wretched place… not you. My life is a battlefield, these scares are irrefutable evidence. What my pride wouldn't allow me to say back in Mute City was… goodbye."

He pressed his palm against my chest immediately after. An enormous gust of wind came from within his palm and, against my will, I found myself being sucked into the warm hole he created. I heard the devil whisper one last word before I got dragged into the unknown.

"Kyle", Felix began.

"I won't let you survive this time."

The shining light spat me out into the darkness and vanished right before my eyes. I sound myself at the top of a mountain, which was a neighbor to a vast forest. There was a river near me that moved so unsettling. I could see a rundown shack made of wood and a nurturing tree right in the middle of it all. Just to the right of the wooden shack was a grave with the name Rosario Vega carved into the stone.

I was home. Why was I home?! Kyle could have made that warp gate take me anywhere in the world... so why bring me to this house of sorrow? Why bring me back to this horrible place?

I lacked companionship. I missed Zeke; I wished that he was here with me right now. But I had hurt him so badly, so much that he bled from the pain. All he wanted was to be with me and I turned him down. What kind of monster would deliberately hurt his only childhood friend? Maybe Kyle was right about me. I always push good things away from me. I push them all away: Nyru, Zeke, Johnny and even Kyle.

Another piercing thought entered my mind; in just ten minutes, Kyle would suffer a tragic death by the hands of Felix Crown. I remembered that question that Kyle asked me just a couple days ago. He asked me if I had any morals—he asked me if I had any self made law that I would never bring myself to break. I was unable to answer that question before, but now I finally think I realized the answer. I finally realized what my morals were. I slowly rose to my feet; on my birthday I realized the code that I would never break.

The warp gate was closed but Kyle's scent was distilled in the open air. I used the trail he carelessly left behind to make my way back to that wretched cave—to make my way back to imminent danger.

As I ran to rescue Kyle I quickly realized the answer to that strange question I asked earlier; why did Kyle bring me back home? The forbidden cave where the devil dwelled was not too far from my own home. I believe the reason he brought me here was so that, if I should choose to fight by his side, then I would not be too far away. Or maybe the locations of these two structures were of pure coincidence and his action was completely selfless. Regardless of the reason, I could not just leave him be.

I ran as fast as my legs would permit and refused to yield to the increasingly excruciating pain of fatigue. I soon found myself by his gates, exhausted and out of breath. As I ventured deeper into the cave I found greater evidence of battle. The splattered blood across the wall was an irrefutable sign of struggle. The soldiers who valued their lives were all gone. They were laid out on the ground as lifeless and motionless as the bullets that had destroyed them. I walked into the heart of the battlefield in search of my best friend. There was a large trail of blood about thirty feet long that caught my attention. What I saw at the end of that bloody trail brought me so close to tears.

In the end of that bloody trail was Kyle's body: cold, mangled, exhausted, sweating, bleeding, and crying from the pain of it all. Felix Crown was right there behind him, ready to deliver the killing blow.

"Where did you send the kid", Felix questioned impatiently.

Kyle's feet were immobilized so he crawled to salvation, like some undying machine.

Again he asked: "Where is Chase Vega? Where is Chase! Where did you send the kid?"

Felix tossed Kyle to the ground like garbage. The devil began to torture my best friend in the most inhumane of ways. He bashed Kyle's skull into the sturdy pavement, over and over again; demanding that same question. In secret, I clenched my belligerent fist and grinded my teeth. More and more I began to notice the life fading from Kyle's eyes. I softly climbed out the shadow in the same manner as before. With courage I said:

"Is it me you're looking for?"

Chapter Ten

Clash of the Titans

No more can I bear that copious thought of loosing someone very dear to me.

"Is it me you're looking for", I shouted to the devil.

"We'll look no further!"

I ran to Kyle's company and struck the devil's face with such immeasurable intensity. Felix crashed into the ground afar, and I turned to comfort Kyle.

He was breathing so shallow, "Are you there", I whispered.

I shook his body delicately and patiently, as if I was waking my big brother from a deserving slumber. I carefully turned him around to see if his face was still there. His mouth was filled with blood, his bones seemed misshapen; yet his fists were still hot with such immense and undying anger. He casually whipped away the blood from his face as if it were sweat. He made an attempt to rise to his feet but the pain in his abdomen quickly pinned him to submission. Kyle's lips were tightly clasped. His pride wouldn't allow his lips to express words of gratitude so my act of selflessness and kindness went unpraised, much like before. This was a very common behavior for this man. And the simple fact that he remained common assured his survival. My mind had less to be troubled with.

He coughed out the remaining blood and said with a soft and agonizing breath, "Why did you come here?"

"If I didn't come I would surely risk a betrayal of my morals", I confessed.

"I came all the way here to protect you from Felix."

"Do you remember that time, not so long ago, when you asked me if I had any morals in which I lived by? You asked if I had any self made rules that I would never disobey. I was unable to answer that question before. Well... today I found my morals. My moral is to protect the ones I love. I've lost too many good people in life's lonely road. That's why I'm here; to protect you. I won't turn my back on you; I won't let anymore of my friends die. I can use the glove's power—let me steal your pain, all of it, just like I've done many times before."

I shut my eyes and reached out my hand to touch Kyle's face and prepared to extract the pain into my own body, as I reached to touch his flesh, he grabbed my hand and stopped me right on the spot.

"No, not this time", said Kyle with a trembling voice.

"Let me endure this pain alone. You are a much better person then I am, Chase. You are beyond me. I haven't been completely honest with you; the truth is... I use to scornfully kiss my teeth at the slightest mentioning of your name. I used such hateful words to blacken your good name. You—you took what were rightfully mine, Leader-One's glove."

I looked at my hands to see that glove that my grandpa gave me as he was passing away, that glove that they killed my mother trying to find, the same irremovable glove that my father cursed me to wear for all eternity.

"That same glove was worn by my hero, Dante the great. Because of your mother, the glove recognizes you as a native and is bonded with your skin forever. I spent my entire life training and training. I deserve a reward—I deserve to have the most powerful glove. I was by far the most qualified, but it was wasted on someone as weak as you. It wasn't long until I devised the plan of simply killing you and cutting off your hands to claim my sot out prize. I disguised my intentions under the alias of divine justice and morality. And so I came on that quiet night, with the courage to do what I'd contemplated for so long. You were much weaker than I thought. I was about to kill you, kind friend, when suddenly, he came! Your guardian angel came to your rescue. It was the spirit of my idol, Dante the great. Very soon I found myself fighting someone that I absolutely adored-- someone that I studied and wanted to be just like. My all-time hero quickly turned his sword against me. I fled only to encounter you the following day. I thought you would turn your back on me and let those monsters kill me; I wished that you would, but you showed more compassion than I did. More compassion then I could have ever mustered. I saved you from the Panoptic Bruiser not as an act of good moral, but rather a zealous notion to clear my guilty conscience. I hated myself the more I got to know you. "I was about to kill a beautiful boy", I thought to myself over and over. Even till this day you continue to prove your kind heartedness and commendable sense of moral judgment. I cursed you and told you never to return here but you disobeyed my inaccurate command and you risked your life and returned. Kind friend you returned, not to ease the pain of a guilty conscience as I had done in the past. You acted selflessly, not to purchase a ticket to heaven but simply because it was the right thing to do. I'm sorry that I hurt you. Don't look me unkindly. If my departing whispers could travel to the past then I would have stopped myself from ever rescuing you from the Panoptic Bruiser. Yes, I would have allowed him to give you death, and with it that perfect lie that you searched your entire life for."

Kyle finished his heartbreaking confession and it left me feeling shattered, awkward and uneasy. I was very silent, and attended to nothing other than my own thoughts. I loved him until this moment.

I could feel Felix Crown's breath on the back of my head.

"There's nothing special about you", he began.

"There never was. What he was truly after since day one was your gloves."

"Is that not the same thing you're after", I rudely questioned.

"Humans are cruelest always to themselves", he began.

"He was your best friend, I'm sorry that he hurt you. But could you imagine what he must have felt? Hurting the people that we care about most is something all living creatures have trouble dealing with. Unclench your fist child, no enemy lies here. Your heart is racing, so many bitter emotions clashing against each other like jag edged swords. I sense anger and rage greatest of all, am I correct? You're slowly killing yourself on the inside. I've found the solution to heartache. Trust me, join me, take my hand and we can unlock the holy trinity. It will destroy this world, yes, but with it all those painful emotions you and everyone else in existence feels every passing second. But most importantly you'll be given love. Let's take the next step of evolution; a practical step towards world peace. Let's merge all minds and souls into one. Together we will create a white canvas filled with nothingness and there you will be taken care of, trust me. Happiness lies just outside these earthly gates"

"Those thoughts are not my own", I said.

"My answer is still no, you made me an orphan. You stole the life of someone priceless to me. I will be the one who destroys you!"

He chuckled quietly to himself and then said, "Kyle Bison was the best."

"I defeated him with ease, the evidence is right there... and there. People spend their entire life training to kill me. Foolish boy, what makes you think you can compare? What makes you think you can do what so many have died trying to do?"

I stood still and growingly doubtful of my own powers. Instead of replying I cracked my muscles and prepared myself for the fight of my life. "It was all up to me now", I thought.

"The fate of the entire world is in my hands. The spotlight shined on this battlefield. The weeping spirits of the fallen carefully gathered themselves, right here in the stage of glory, to witness their avenger kill the undying murderer; the cause of their dismay. I could not dismiss their wish, for they were once my childhood friends. There invisible expressions were hidden all around me in plain sight."

Felix stood in an intimidating fighter's stance and said with a cold whisper:

"This is the end of you, Chase India Vega!"

I tried to keep calm and hoped that all the stories that I heard about this man were untrue. I wouldn't look him in the eye or breathe his breath. I nodded my head in an o so formal way, and that marked the beginning of Felix Crown's brutal assault on me.

He moved as swiftly as a god of war. Every lethal strike was with such absolute precision, aimed carefully at every vital organ in my body; he wielded the intention to destroy me with every strike. There were no mistakes—no errors, no fruitless attacks. Every contact was devastating. I desperately tried to avoid each blow; it was as if his hands were sharp edged swords. And like a sword fight, any false move could kill. If I kept fighting like this I would die very, very soon. He delivered another precise and devastating blow and I crashed into the strong rock floor. I thought he would finish me off right there while I lay motionless on the ground. But he showed what I call warriors compassion. He kept his distance and didn't attack until I got back on my two feet. I was dizzy and light headed too; I took some time to catch my breath. He came closer and closer to me, until our noses almost touched. I immediately turned away from his haunting yellow eyes, just like the deceased soldiers told me to.

"Why are you doing this", he said.

And I replied with an unsteady voice, "Because it's the right thing to do."

"Really", he questioned.

"How many people are living inside your head? Whose thoughts are you obeying so honorably? Let me ask you this, if those scattered thoughts are truly yours, then what will you do if a miracle occurs and you somehow manage to kill me? Will you return to that dark ally and wait till you die? All the members of the Oddity dislike you, I'm sure you've overheard some of their careless whispers. The woman of your dreams has sworn to hate you for all eternity. Even your oldest childhood friend, Zeke, has had a change of heart. I can't blame them… after what you've done. Now tell me what is your reason for living? Is it to continue searching for your dead mother?"

I was overwhelmed with rage and so close to tears. I struck him repeatedly; over and over again. He recovered so quickly from the attack and began his verbal assault.

"Shall we dig further into your discarded memories?"

"The gun was pointed at you! Don't you remember? You're mother gave her life for you. You're the one who should have died; your father thinks so too. You never even told her you loved her."

He dug his hands deeper and deeper into the doors I kept safely locked away in the deepest trenches and darkest pit of my soul and ripped it right out of me. He opened the doors of my sins and released all my greatest nightmares. They spewed out from within me like a horde of black locust. All my darkest sins were carefully noted. His haunting eyes could see through closed doors and deceptive smiles. No, it was written on my face in plain English. Yes, the names of the one's that I've wronged are right there in my eyes.

I fought the devil with all I had. There was so much rage bottled up inside me, if I could somehow turn it into physical energy it still wouldn't be nearly enough to stop Felix Crown. Nothing can stop him; bullets, arrows, knives, daggers and even sharp edged swords all bend when they near his wretched flesh! The worst feeling in the world is giving something all that you've got and failing miserably. I've given it all I've got already. I just can't beat him. I was overwhelmed with a sense of hopelessness.

In time I lost the will to fight. And with good reasons I wished for death.

The eternal burden of this world seemed to disapprove! His intent was to persuade me to help bring the realization of his plans. When he realized that I was giving up, he turned to his secret weapon, Kyle Bison. He grabbed Kyle's immobilized body by the skull and turned him so that we looked each other face to face. Then, he did the unimaginable. He started to crush Kyle's skull.

Kyle gave a heart shattering cry for help. My eyes open wide with fear.

"Stop it! Stop it", I shouted.

I wished that strength was measured only by ones will. If that were so then no supernatural being could prevent me from rescuing my best friend! My war torn body did not allow me. There was no word that could describe his agony, or the helplessness that I felt. I think I could hear his skull cracking. I then recalled that painful vision I had of Kyle passing away. I read the book of time over and over, and proved unable to change a single word of it. I shouted much louder than before.

"Stop it you monster! You're gonna kill him! Stop it Felix! Stop it! Stop it! Stop it! For god's sake please stop. "

Again, my words passed thru deaf ears. Kyle was dying slowly and ever so painfully. I wish I could take his place. I shouted and shouted but my sorrow only fed Felix's smile--and he smiled wider and wider. There was a raging storm brewing inside me.

My world was at the edge of destruction. Just as I was about to give up hope—just when my enduring heart was about to be overflow and burst into a million peaces--

The ancient spirit that lived deep inside me awakened! My unstoppable guardian angel had returned! He stood behind me like a colossal titan, and challenged the eternal god of war.

"Leave him be", my guardian angel demanded.

"Dante the great", Felix said with excitement.

He threw Kyle to the side so discourteously.

The spirit of Dante flew to me with tremendous speed and then stopped instantly; his sudden halt blew a gust of wind that blinded me for just a moment. When my eyes reopened, I was frightened that he looked me face to face and wore an antagonizing expression. He aimed at me with such hate and disappointment; I took a step backwards in fear that he would turn his sword against me and strike me down. After seconds of awkward silence he unclasped his lips and every breath marked cruel insult to my name.

"You are seriously weak kid", he whispered dispassionately.

"You have single handedly brought shame to our proud nation! You lack both physical and emotional strength. You would have lived then lost that life all in the same hour; that is, if you were born in olden times (they kill weak children). Your existence has proved to be our nation's greatest error. You have shamed us, forsaken us! We were the elites! Our strength even challenged that of the gods. Your blood is our own, but your mind and heart are both orphans.

I'm getting very tired of defending you. If it wasn't for her insisting then I would have let you perish years ago. It is I who must undo this eternal burden. Now let me rest in your flesh."

Dante did something that I thought was impossible. He pulled my body away from my soul. No, it didn't hurt at all. The entire procedure felt like cold water crashing against my flesh; and it happened just as swiftly. He replaced my soul with his own. He sat down on that chair that my soul knew so fondly, and then controlled my body like a lifeless puppet. I was outside of my own body; it was strange. I was locked out of my house and watching carefully though the window. I felt like an intruder of my own body. I wondered maybe if this was what death felt like.

Dante carefully examined my body and said softly to himself:

"This body is much weaker than the last one."

Dante separated his legs and bent his knees. His left hand was positioned in a defensive manner; his right hand was the striker. Felix crouched slightly too. His right hand was closest to his heart and his opposite hand was held like a shield. The two had an identical fighter's stance. The similarity was so great that they could be mistaken for a mirror image of each other. Which ignited the question, how much history does Felix and Dante share?

"How many times must I kill you", Felix questioned.

"Time brings great change", Dante replied.

"You have not changed the variables in the equation. The solution will also remain unchanged", said Felix Crown

"Can't you sense the immense difference in our level of power? You're gamboling a child's life this time. You watched your entire clan die right before your eyes. When they needed you the most you were gone. You should be flattered, the young and the old shouted your name like a holy chant. "Dante will come soon, Dante will punish you". But you never came to their rescue! You're upset because I killed you and took everything you knew and loved. You're upset because the student surpassed the master and inadvertently destroyed your good name. Stop hiding under the pretentious shroud of morality, justice and self-righteousness. Your undying soul continues to return because you want what every victim of murder wants, revenge! You should never have said no to my offer, so long ago. You have only yourself to blame."

Felix verbally strikes the weakest point of the heart long before the initial conflict. Dante remained as solid as a rock. He didn't let Felix's cruel words get to him at all. And that simple gesture proved that he was much stronger than I could ever be.

"You haven't changed a bit", Dante said with a smile.

"You're still the little ocean eyed boy that hates losing. You were my best friend! You were the only outsider that was allowed into the sacred Zodant tribe. Do you remember the first time we met in the coliseum? We defeated them all, and then the matchmakers forced us to fight each other. A million years have gone by since then, our bodies have become corpses. Yet we still stand face to face, in a different coliseum.

I'll never forget the sound of your voice when you told me your childhood dream. Do you still want to grow wings and taste the sky?

I saved you from the monsters and then bid farewell in times of peace! I didn't know they would do that to you, not your own people. I left you in good company, so I thought. I once drowned myself in guilt. If my voice could reach back to the past then I would have told myself to never leave your side. I even used my glove's power to steal the pain from you. But the memories were still there. I once drowned myself in guilt. I regret nothing now because in the end nobody, not even I, could have saved you from yourself. O kind friend, come, and let me destroy the monster that you've become."

"You are just as much a fool as you are blind", said Felix.

Felix released another black moon from the palm of his hand and aimed it at Dante. Dante slapped it away just when it was about to collide into him. The black moon aged his left hand by a thousand years. Now I feared that my left hand would look misshapen forever. Dante used his right hand to soothe his opposite hand; by doing so he was able to dispatch the curse and heal himself. Dante then raised his hand and swung it in a downward motion. Suddenly, meteors fell from the sky like fiery rain. They all piled upon a common enemy. The match was far from over.

Dante bolted towards Felix and just as soon as Felix walked out of the rubble, he struck him square in the face. Felix and Dante moved just the same... the way they ducked and weaved punches was perfectly symmetrical. Every blow was aimed precisely at a pressure point or vital organ. They were clearly the worlds finest. I felt like a spectator watching an Olympic event. The battle that would determine the fate of humanity waged on. Both supernatural fighters began to tire. Fatigue and exertion had struck its target. They stood on the opposite ends of the battle field, honoring each other just a moment to catch their breath and regain their strength. They were equals in every meaning of the word. This civil conflict could have gone on for days.

I suppose Felix was the first to realize this, he summoned a warp gate. I was up to my chin in curiosity.

"What could possibly come out of that pit", I wondered.

Felix reached into the unknown and dragged out a weapon. It was a long hard wood spear; it seemed like such a primitive weapon for such an important fight. I turned my head to the other end of the battlefield and saw that Dante also summoned a warp gate. From his he dragged a dark black spear with a peculiar series of colorful chimes located on the opposing end of the blade. It was the weapon of choice for the Zodant clan. Each ring represented your rank as a clan member and makes a unique noise when they collide into each other. The song of the rings warns enemies that a powerful force is nearing; I was thought this by my mother.

The two dashed toward each other and collided with the same intensity as two speeding trains. They offensively swung there spears in such a brilliant manner. Every swing was nearly fatal. An attack that missed was so close that it would just brush against the tip of the nose or speed by the horizon of your shoulder blade. Even a defensive technique was silently awaiting an even stronger offensive strike. The ancient warrior gambled with my life for one final dance with the devil. What would become of me if he proved unsuccessful? Will he allow my soul to return? Can a soul return to a perished body? Soon, very soon, this will all be over. When that happens will I be forced to wonder this earth like some unseen spirit of the dead? Uncertainty chilled me to the very bone.

The match waged on. And Felix's blade gruesomely slashed against Dante's flesh—my flesh. I was at the edge of my feet with my eyes open wide. Blood gushed…

"This is your third attempt", Felix shouted.

"We trained together! I mastered everything you thought me! What makes you think you can beat me?"

Dante lost his balance and stumbled backwards. He planted his spear firmly on the ground and used it as a balancing cane. It seemed like the match was over, it seemed like my life was no more. Felix has proved to be victorious again. And then—to my surprise, Dante the great stood again on his two feet. There was still some fight left in him. He used the gloves power to create a flame, and with that scorching flame be patched up his giant cut. He shouted from the agony. The pain must have been tremendous. He was a true warrior, I didn't have the heart or the will to go thru with that procedure. He managed to stop the bleeding. For a moment the room stood silent.

"I didn't teach you everything", Dante said with a painful smile.

"There were three Zodant techniques that I was forbidden from teaching to outsiders. I'll defeat you this time. The equation is not the same because… the child carries my bloodline and the child's strong willed mother has been with me the entire time!"

The burden that I've been carrying for so long had suddenly gotten much lighter. I smiled. My mom was helping me the entire time. Sorrow had become washed away, and I didn't feel so alone.

"Now", said Dante.

"Let me show you the sacred Zodant techniques that I was forbidden from teaching you!"

Dante separated his legs further and crouched even lower to the ground. His hands were thrown into the air, mimicking a curving motion. He twisted his waist, like how dancers do when they begin a spin. And from the top of his lungs he shouted, "Hurricane style."

An explosion of shimmering light swarmed around him. His eyes turned red, his fingernails became sharp like knives, and black hairs filled his body. He was half man half wolf.

This ancient warrior had quickly taken the Zodant blood passed on from my mother's genes and the werewolf gene passed on by my father and turned it into one unique and lethal combination. While holding the spear, he began a series of spins and kicks. He moved so quickly that he created a barrier from his own attack. He neared Felix Crown, spinning faster and faster. Even Felix with his godly speed could not dodge the full blunt of the attack. Dante reached Felix at arm's length and began cutting him more and more with that devastating spin. Felix was covered in blood. Dante then introduced the second sacred technique of the Zodant trib. With a deep voice Dante shouted, "Raging storm!"

Immediately a hurricane of scorching flames surrounded him, generated and fueled by the friction of his unnatural spinning motion. Gales of fiery wind tiered through the stormy air. Felix had his back against the wall with nowhere to run to. The flames pierced him sharply; and burned away every inch of his flesh—

Dante continued the attack. Felix was nothing more than bones and red flesh. "Felix had to be dead, nobody could survive that", I kept telling myself.

Dante stopped the attack, still spinning slightly. He grabbed his spear with both hands and leaped into the air to deliver the final blow.

"This is it", I though.

"It's all over now!"

Only bones and red flesh remained, but Felix was still alive and standing. He grabbed his weapon and forced it into Dante's stomach. And then he gave a sinister smile. Dante coughed out a lot of blood. He was suspended in the air and layed on top of a razor sharp blade.

"You can't beat me", he whispered to Dante

"The Zodant clan is no more!"

Despite our combined efforts we simply could not defeat the final boss. Felix would find a way to activate the holy trinity and with it... everything we have come to love will perish. My vision had at last come true.

I could see Dante loosing strength, the evidence was written plainly on his face. He was being overcome by death. Then suddenly, with the last of his fleeting energy, Dante raised his spear and the sharp blade leaned down to kiss Felix.

Dante twisted the spear and separated Felix's chin from the rest of his head. The two friends froze for a moment, like a tragic painting. And then fell to the ground. The two titans layed dead and motionless, like exhausted children laying beneath the shade. I stood there quietly and watched them doze away.

I wondered if I was dead as well.

The silence wasn't so bad.

I slowly walked to where my body laid, and felt sad when I saw all that blood. Death was all around me: Kyle, Felix, and Dante were all someplace else.

The spirit of Dante softly touched my shoulder. I turned my head then struggled to ask a very difficult question.

"Am I dead", I said while stuttering slightly.

"You're trapped between the narrow gulf that separates life from death", he replied.

"The glove has the ability to heal, you know this. But it cannot heal those on the distant shore--what's already dead. Your heart rate is so low that it's virtually undetectable. But your mind is working just fine. If you enter your body but lack the will to survive then your heart rate will seize and you will die. If you choose to live, and fight for survival, then your heart rate will remain alive and the glove will begin to slowly heal you. Whether you live or die is all up to you, it always has been."

"I can protect you no more", he said in a departing whisper.

"Chase, you are the last of our kind, promise me that you will grow big and strong. I haven't slept in a million years. Let me rest my weary soul."

My guardian angel walked thru the cave wall and slowly vanished. For moments, I watched my body sleeping calm and soundly. The difference between a gift and a curse is simple; a gift you can return but a curse you must live with forever. The loathsome curse that my father infected upon me had been lifted. I looked at my hands and I didn't feel sad any longer because the gloves were gone. For the first time in twelve years I could see my naked hands, feel the warmth from my flesh, the breeze passing through the spaces between my fingers, and the roughness from sharp edged rocks and stones. I smiled and grew infant eyes. We, as humans, tend to ignore the simplest things; the indescribable sensation of touch and feel never strike us with value until. Only when that sensation is gone do we crave it. A very serious thought flashed across my mind. I thought of abandoning the world that I knew and simply walking through that stubborn wall and vanishing to the same place Dante was. I wanted to join my people, to be accepted. I wanted to be home, not in a dark alley or a house of sorrow. The entire Zodant clan was just outside these earthly gates. My mother was there too. If I left I wouldn't feel so alone. My journey would be over. Leaving this world was the smartest thing to do. I gave my lifeless shell a warm embrace.

I entered my body with the courage to continue living. And for a second I saw only darkness. "Perhaps I waited too long", I thought.

I then slowly opened my eyes and could see the light. My war torn body was healing, slowly. I crawled to where my best friend lay. I shook him gently until he awoke.

"It's all over Kyle", I said with a soft voice.

But the danger grows…

Kyle grew increasingly concerned. The greatest level of fear covered his face.

"Felix isn't dead", he shouted.

"The glove gives him immortality! As long as he wears those gloves he can just recover himself!"

Felix was at that gulf between life and death. He could recover himself the same way I did! With my guardian angel gone forever, I soon found myself wearing the same frantic expression Kyle did. I slowly turned my neck and could see the devil's skin beginning to return.

Kyle reached into the holster that was tied around his leg. He pulled out a sharp knife and clumsily walked to where Felix's immobilized body layed. He fell to the ground, right where the devil was, and began to cut off Felix's hands. He inhumanly chipped away at Felix's bones as if it were ice. There was blood everywhere, the very sight of it made me sick to my stomach. I tried to look away but was then greeted by the sound of bones cracking. Kyle managed to cut off one hand and began to work his way towards the second. Felix now laid in a pool of his own blood. Kyle's hands were painted red.

Again, but with less hesitation, Kyle began chipping away at Felix's other hand. He hacked away like a butcher. Kyle proved unyielding to the scent and sound of blood and bones.

"This was wrong", I thought to myself.

"Even convicts and animals have their lives taken in a more humane manner."

The blood continued to poor. Just as I thought things couldn't get any more gruesome, the unimaginable happened.

Felix awoke!

His right hand was torn off and his left hand was hanging by a brittle thread. Felix released a demonic moan and bashed his skull into Kyle Bison's, over and over. Kyle flinched and bled immediately after the impact. I instinctively grabbed Felix and tried to restrain him the best way I knew how. He was bound tightly to me; I just had to buy enough time until Kyle finished the cruel deed. The devil calmly turned his head and looked me eye to eye. Kyle tore off his last hand! Felix looked deep into my very soul the life faded from his eyes like a dying bulb.

I released his corpse and Kyle stripped the gloves from Felix's severs hands and reaped the reward. There were tears in my eyes. I've never watched a man die before. I've committed murder on this day. But what bothered me most—what made me overwhelmed with sadness was that this could have just as easily happened to me. My best friend Kyle had very serious thoughts of ripping my arms off and collecting my gloves, the same way he did with Felix. Death changes a man, in ways I find difficult to describe. After this moment I saw Kyle in a new light, I found it impossible to determine which was Kyle Bison's true self.

"We have to go now", Kyle shouted.

I had myself firmly planted on the ground. I just gave a moment to calm my rapid beating heart. Then, very slowly, I dragged myself to my feet.

"C'mon Chase we have to leave now", he insisted.

He grabbed my hand and tugged me away!

"Have you forgotten about the bomb", he shouted.

There was only one way out and Felix sealed it soon after we entered. Kyle looked at his watch, which was synchronized to the bomb's detonation. There wasn't much time remaining. We banged at the bolder and tried to create the slightest opening so we can crawl out of. Hopelessness grew with the passage of time. Even if we managed to break through the seal and ran as fast as our human legs would allow, we could not escape the blast radius. Our grave has been sealed. We can escape death no longer.

The candle of our will burned ever so dimly. Just as it was about to go out, the boulder that sealed our graves turned to rubble. Right on the other side of that wall was Johnny Sage, the man who released us. He carried Kyle and I in each hand like children, and with his jet pack, simply flew out of harm's way. I listened closely to the timer on Kyle's watch. Tick, tick, tick—it seemed to be getting louder. Then suddenly it paused for just a moment, and then the alarm went off; then the bomb soon after. Whiteness blinded my eyes and the heat proved to be increasingly difficult. The explosion spat us just outside the cave's entrance. The explosion inflicted no further damage to us. The eerie cave then fell in on itself, sealing it forever!

We came with a hundred soldiers and in just moments that number drastically reduced to a small handful of survivors. They laughed and congratulated each other for surviving the impossible. Johnny Sage went to attend to the remaining soldiers. Kyle Bison's glove was not like my own; it lacked the ability to heal, so he was immediately rushed to receive medical attention. He gave me a carefree smile and then bid a moment's farewell. As for me...well...there was no need for me anymore. Felix Crown was finally gone. The Oddities have proved successful. All was well with the world.

Everyone went their separate ways, and again I began to march along that lonely road. I retraced the footprints that the war machine carelessly left behind. I hoped that I would find my old friend Zeke somewhere along this road. I hoped that god looked after him. I hoped that I would find him soon because the condition I left him in before made him an easy target for scavengers and predators. He was my oldest childhood friend. I wanted to mend his broken heart and show him love once more. And then, maybe, play that game we both like so much.

Several military vehicles zoomed right past me. I didn't think much of it at first, until they all symmetrically slammed on the breaks and blocked my path. I continued walking in my normal paste. When I grew nearer, I saw a much too familiar face.

"What will you do now", questioned Dr. Osco.

"I'm gunna go look for my friend", I said.

Our shoulders brushed against each other. Just as I was seconds away from walking past him and through the barricade, I felt a sharp pain on my neck like the bite from a mosquito. I plucked the insect from the back of my neck and was surprised to see that it wasn't a mosquito at all. It was more like a tiny needle. I turned the needle around and in fine print it said "Property of Osco laboratory." Immediately my muscles tightened. My legs grew heavier.

"What have you done", I demanded.

Osco smiled then said, "I'm afraid I cannot allow you to leave, not this time."

"The drug has paralyzed your body, correct? Soon, very soon, you will fall into a deep sleep. But now that I have your undivided attention I think its best that I tell you the entire truth. My father Dr. Eugene Osco had an unnatural thirst for learning. He didn't waste his time on relationships or interactions. This new world was something enticing to him. Something complex he wanted to take apart and rebuild. Felix, who was a strong collaborator, showed him the power's of the glove. Something that was unimaginable in the previous world. More importantly, Felix told him, in great detail, about the destruction and rebirth of all living creatures. It was a process Felix called, The Holy Trinity. Felix gave his own hairs to help Osco create super soldiers who aid him in activating the Holy Trinity. Those disciples—those allies of Felix were called Project Oddity.

"No, that can't be true", I said in disbelief.

"You misunderstood your father's experiments."

"Incorrect", he said emotionlessly.

"Dr. Eugene Osco fathered no children! He invested all his time on his studies alone. When death came knocking on his door, he simply made a perfect clone of himself. In that clone lies all the knowledge that he collected throughout his years. I am that perfect clone. I won't let Leader-One's glove hid from me any longer. I will combine all three sacred gloves and destroy this world. That is the true meaning of project Oddity!"

I could feel the effects of the drug taking its toll. I didn't even have the strength to call for help. My guardian angel was gone forever. The last person that would help me was Zeke, and I wasn't even sure if he was dead or alive. With my last breath I cursed the man that started it all.

"Damn you Osco! We trusted you! We obeyed your every command like loyal dogs. We even gave a toast to your name."

My vision became drastically impaired.

"I hold no personal grudge against you", he said.

"This is all in the name of science."

My heart harbored such vulgar emotions. The light fled and everything turned black. They dragged me discourteously into the military vehicle and shipped me to their secrete construct.

Chapter Eleven

Eternal Devastation

I slept for what appeared to be a thousand years, and in every influential second of my slumber…nightmares came. In the realm of dreams, an eternity of sorrow would pass you in just an hour's time. I was tortured by painful memories over and over again. I stared into the eyes of the devil; I wandered if this was the end result. I should have paid more attention to what the talkative soldier had to say. I lost my carefree smile long, long ago. Love seemed like an uncertain memory.

I slowly became aware of myself. The crushing grip that this realm had upon me slowly began to loosen. I was waking up. At last I was finally waking up. Serious thoughts of murder filled my mind. I wanted to destroy that old man for his betrayal. The other realm released me from its clutches. I was spat out, back into the real world.

My eyes opened slightly…

God's light did not great me. I was trapped in a jar filled with thick water. At first glance I saw nothing but darkness and obscure images. I assumed I was in a laboratory, because only here could one find a collection of such advanced equipments. I watched through the glass like a prisoner.

Then, something caught my eyes; something peculiar and out of place. Directly in front of me were the bones of a deceased animal. I wasn't shocked to see death; no, death I knew quite fondly. But what became increasingly disturbing was that this animal's bones were not scattered; it didn't die in the wild, but instead it died in a sleeping position. The bones seemed almost preserved. It was as if the animal died while waiting for something.

I felt a terrible foreboding.

I removed my breathing mask and punched my way out the glass prison. The thick water flowed beneath my feet like rivers and streams. I walked carefully towards that neglected pile of bones. As I inched closer I soon realized that this was no wild animal. It had a collar around its neck. Slowly I turned the collar to see the name that this still, discarded, and lonely animal answered to. The animal's name was Zeke; my life's finest companion.

All sound faded. My heart raced.

At long last my greatest nightmares have been realized to such horrifying perfection. My hands were shaking. I fell to my knees as if my feet lacked balance. I burst to tears and embraced his cold and lifeless bones. I wept uncontrollably. I shouted at him to wake up and come back to me. I even cursed at him for leaving me right when I needed him most. "How could he leave me now, after all that we've shared", I questioned.

I shouted till my throat grew horse with rage. I wished that my magical gloves could break the rules just once and somehow give life to the dead. I wish he could have taken me with him. I'm truly grateful that fate brought us together, but now I cursed the fate that would not allow me to die alongside you. He should have smuggled me away to paradise. I would have quietly accepted. I would have hidden in the blanket of his hair until we arrived. I laid right there on the dirty ground and cradled his icy bones in my arms. Zeke waited an eternity for me to return. Like a loyal dog he watched over his dead master until finally un-favoring death came to claim his own life. For hours I laid there, soon day turned to night and night to day.

Two days have come and gone unnoticed; and soon, very soon I greatly hungered for revenge. Only then did I lift myself off the floor and bid a silent farewell to my oldest childhood friend. After moments of wondering blindly in the dark I soon came across an elevator. The elevator was protected by a thin steel fence. There was a button on my right hand side, about waist high. I pressed the button to activate the machine but it did not reply. There was a lack of power. And it was that same absence of electricity that disturbed my eternal slumber. I ripped the steel cage apart like some savage beast. I then crawled up the elevator shaft. Every thrust onward was fueled by bitter revenge. I crawled one hundred yards in pure darkness. Finally, I freed myself from the underground laboratory and crawled my way out of the repulsive dirt like a living corpse. I was dirty, alone, cold and sweating but more importantly, I still stood tall. I showed courage. But what my eyes were to witness next was truly devastating…

My eyes opened wide with fear and great disbelief. Mute City was swallowed by darkness. The trees were the color of death and dug into the soil like a marking of a grave. The toxic stench of rotten corpses filled the air; it was a stench so overpowering that I was forced to shield my nose immediately. Homes and churches were engulfed by flames. Skyscrapers were reduced to rubble. Upon my un-deaf ears lay the adiposity of the city's mornings. My ears grew deaf from the despairing shrieks of lingering souls. I wished that my eyes could spit out the wretched images. With dragging steps I walked deeper into the great city of silence. A soldier saves the world but returns home to fight another. The bones of men trampled under my foot. Bodies were pilled upon bodies. There was no red carpet, well rehearsed band, cheers or confetti to welcome me. No beautiful princess waiting for me at the end of my journey. My labor had proved to be frightfully unrewarded. Even at this distance, receiving this vision was increasingly difficult. The city itself was… sordid, and as I grew nearer, the stench of rotten corpses also grew ten folds; all criticizes were diseased and dangerously thin from starvation.

My legs grew heavy—I walked further.

Some people sat outside their porches, and looked up at the sky as if they were awaiting their savior. Others laid thoughtlessly right by the foul-smelling sewers and rats. I walked by that dark alley that Zeke and I once lived in. The secret construct, we use to call it. I glanced at the countless markings on the wall. Each mark represented a life that I could not save. Suddenly thousands of images pierced into the back of my mind. The voices and faces of the people I could not save during my slumber flashed through my mind like photographs. I could see through their eyes, I could hear their playful laughers, I could read their thoughts seconds before they perished. It was as if I had known them all my entire life. In moments I felt the heart ache of a thousand years. My heart too grew heavy. I built the walls around my heart even higher.

The moon's shine was smeared by darkness. No heavenly stars hung above me, only grey and gloomy clouds. I walked deeper into this forsaken city like a lost soul. Still in disbelief I wondered:

"Who could have caused this? Felix Crown was dead. To assure it we even ripped away his source of power. I was absent during times of peace. I obeyed all of their rules. What could have gone wrong? Where is the love they promised me?

With a heavy heart I marched passed the remains of the place where Nyru lived. I passed the sacred territory that the juveniles once played in, and was welcomed by the eerie laughter of ghostly children.

It was then that a disturbing thought entered my mind.

"Perhaps Kyle was the one to blame for all of this. He expressed to me his love for fighting in such frightful detail. He was going to kill me, his best friend, and cut off both my hands so he can selfishly harness the power it holds. His greatest dream is to be strong like Dante & Felix. He was created for war alone; he spent his entire life training to slay the perfect monster. Now that Felix is no more—perhaps he grew bored in these peaceful times.

I lent them my hands to help drag down Felix Crown from his passionless sovereignty. As a reward he promised me companionship and above all contentment. And I, like the fool that I was, speedily obeyed each lie. The wearisome labor has been done. Now where are all the fine things you promised me? Where is my happiness?

Yes, I'm sure this is your doing. When we killed Felix, I saw you sneakily tuck Felix's gloves deep into your pockets. Kyle must have caused this. Maybe you plotted with Osco to put me into deep slumber. Maybe this was the plan from the very beginning. Dante's glove is the only one that can stop Felix's—I'm the only one that can stop Kyle. Just like Dante killed his best friend, I too would have to claim the life of my dearest companion.

I walked deeper into a path as thin as the city's lifeless pulse. Upon every corner I saw a great plague of sorrow. Cracks in the earth were like hatched tombs of bitter souls. I thought that I had lost my way and somehow stumbled upon hell. Since this was so, I secured my mind with thoughts of heaven. All the buildings had received tremendous damage. But there was one structure that remained virtually unscathed by the passing of time.

There was only one.

A giant male statue towered over me. Its head was held proudly in the sky like a godly symbol of hope. Filled with visceral curiosity, I shuffled my feet to see the face of the god I did not know. The statue wore the face of a child; and just beneath its feet was a protective hound that was equally keen. I was quickly overcome with pity for soon I came to realized that this colossal symbol of hope was I. I was the paladin that was greatly sod after; they had died waiting for me. With no reason to stay, I slowly turned my head and gave a quiet withdrawal.

Immediately my feet were frozen tight by the dreadful recollection of a familiar voice.

"Elliot, Is that you Elliot", questioned the voice masked by shadows.

I turned around slowly, uncertain if it were my own will I was obeying or the will of some witch's spell. I neared myself to that obscure image. Her figure, like my memory, grew clearer with every progressive step. An eerie mist filled the night sky. All grew dreadfully silent as

I took a step into the shroud of shadows. Even as silent as the night was, the civil war of my mind and heart brewed such blatant and inconsolable tempests.

"Chase, don't you remember me", she questioned.

I nodded my head.

"I could never forget you…Nyru."

She had aged, like all living things do, but her beauty was everlasting. Her hair was the color of the morning sky. Her black eyes shined like a pond filled with stars and her lips the sweetest Clementine. Soon I yearned to feel her skin against my own, like subtle currents upon a burning flesh. All these fine thoughts only renewed my greatest regret.

I thought about that night and that unspeakable sin. I could look at her no more. With my head held shamefully to the ground I begged genuinely for forgiveness.

"I wish to fade from view. For my sins I will be ripped into two and dragged deep into the second and ninth rings of hell. And those on earth shall not frown at my unwilling departure. This is that which I possess; my old friends have moved on and lovers un-want me. Our shared memories shape the very facet of my sweetest dreams. My awareness dawns and with light I can see perceptibly. I now prosecute my own actions, yes; for I undeniably brought the instrumentality of reputable concurrent living.

"Speak plainly with your heart, not your mind", she said to me.

I gathered my thoughts into common English.

"Then let me say it more simply", I replied.

"I'm lonely."

"This is what fills my soul. I was alone so I wanted to become one with you. Merging our bodies into one would give me a purpose, or so I thought.

My face was smitten with grief. She placed one finger on the center of my chin and slowly lifted my head to meet her comforting eyes.

"You haven't changed at all", she whispered softly.

"You could not find where your happiness lies, so you sod after the primordial satisfactions of physical pleasures. A moment of kindness served to be the vessel from your discontent. Pain is something all men must endure in the deepest trenches of the heart. The act of living is the acceptance of change. If you're willing to accept that perspective then you were never truly alone."

I looked at Nyru now with a dull expression. The self that resided in my mind faultlessly matched the image standing right before me. Signs of age became increasingly noticeable. There was no doubt that this was the girl that I fell in love with, but what I was dying to discover was, how long have I been gone? In the night, we stood two arm's length away from each other. A silent breeze playfully swept along out hairs.

Finally I mustered the strength to ask her those long suppressed questions.

"Who did this", I asked with a trembling voice.

"A lot can happen in thirty years", she began.

"We have taken a tide for the worst. The evidence is everywhere. Time brings great change, but very few changes smitten requiems and religious dogmas. Why is that? The world of religion controlled my body. Those hypocrites all looked me unkindly! The act was blasphemy. I was unable to abort… You left me as a woman that could not bleed."

"I don't understand what you're talking about", I said with a grain of frustration.

"The answer is preserved in your memory. Now tell me, who did this?

"The actuality is far beyond you", she confessed.

"The truth will crush and devastate you!"

I stood in frustration, and she in dismay of equivalent degree. The silence was increasing, my hands formed two iron fists, I grinded my teeth in annoyance.

"Was Dr. Osco to blame", I asked.

"No", she said.

"Osco died from natural causes just a few short months after Felix was destroyed."

"Was it Kyle Bison", I questioned.

"No", she quickly replied.

"Kyle and the rest of the Oddity members died trying to protect us from…them."

I hung my head in shame. O, how I've misjudged you kind friend. Kyle, sleepless protector of man, may your soul find peace. I tightened my fist and a greater question surfaced.

"Who are they", I demanded.

Again she retreated to that opposing silence. My frustration deepened.

"Felix Crown's death gave birth to a small group of followers." she began.

"They are the oncs who brought eternal devastation upon our land. They call themselves The Enders…"

"Then I'll seek them out and destroy them like they destroyed our land", I shouted.

"I'll do it without Zeke, or Kyle, or Dante! I'll do it all by myself! I won't even bother God this time!"

"I'm afraid it's not that simple", she interrupted.

"You can't just fight your way out of this one. One of the Enders— one of the people responsible… is your own son."

My eyes opened wide with disbelief.

"Chase you were my greatest joy. With you I shared my greatest laughs. I never would have guessed that you would just as quickly turn into my greatest regret. You were lonely—you had no place to turn to so I welcomed you into my home. And like a skilled thief you deceived me and robbed me of my pleasure. I hated myself, but most importantly I hated you, Chase India Vega!

You left me to care for your child alone. He was like you in every way. For that I could not love him, not the child that reminded me of my greatest regret. No child is born evil. As the mother I take full responsibility, yes, I made Elliot truly wretched. I made him the abomination that he is today. It is I you should seek out and destroy."

She burst to tears and I showed my natural lack of compassion by denying her a word or a comforting gesture. In truth, I too was greatly saddened.

I wish that technology controlled every aspect of our lives, so much so that we could undo and erase every facet of human error. I wish that these magical gloves could somehow steal the pain from the entire universe.

"How can I make things right again", I begged.

"Go and find your son Elliot Vega", she said while drying her tears.

"He deserves to meet his father. You must find him and make him change his ways. God knows where he is now."

I did not know where to even begin searching for my son. I wondered if he was angry with me for not being a part of his life. I thought it was ironic; he hated me like I hated my father. I turned my back to the last survivor of my turbulent past. I left without the comfort of a warm embrace or an endearing farewell. I was unsure where to go, with the right road lost; I simply followed the dark pulse of endless sorrow. I walked alone, stripped from the comfort of my fine companions. Not even my shadow followed. I marched further upon that uncertain road and soon I found myself along a dark forest. I pushed away the dying trees and found myself in a forsaken place. The dark pulse of sorrow led me back to my home.

I spent my entire life searching for my dead mother. My own father blames me for the loss of his precious wife. Kyle, Zeke and grandpa were someplace else. All that is good had perished from this world forever.

My once peaceful home had endured even greater destruction. The river by my home grew very thinly; the water flowed like blue thread along an empty ocean bed. I walked to the edge of the cliff and caught sight of a giant basilisk waiting deep beneath the water. Its deadly red eyes glowed menacingly, and nearly turned me to stone. I dropped a large rock into the foot of the waterfall. The monster beneath the water lashed out its powerful tentacles and crushed the rock with ease; it dragged the remains into the bottom of the murky sea and devoured it. The hungry monster squirmed impatiently and by doing so created giant currents that shook the very ground I stood on. The creature imitated a snake's lethal striking position. It looked to me now with those menacing eyes, hoping that I would jump off the cliff next.

I gave it a very serious thought. Seconds turned to minutes, and minutes to hours. Faith's sharp look severed all earthly ties. All my friends were dead; God's given no thought in returning them. Now, I hoped that those in heaven would not un-want me if I chose to join you.

I neared myself to the edge of the cliff. Only half my feet stood on solid ground. I looked down at the monster's anticipating glare. The basilisk promoted each step forward. I harbored no cowardice in my heart. The pain would be tremendous, I know, but the reward even greater. I didn't fear death any more. If I can embrace the one's I love in death, then death must simply be another dream.

I thought of the interesting novel that the Panoptic Bruiser ranted on and on about. The protagonist and I would meet the same fate.

I leaned further towards the cliff. Soon, very soon, my life would be thru.

My eyes shall never see the light of day. With the last of my living thoughts I recalled the greatest thrills of my life; I recalled my mother's nurture and the heartwarming song of emotions.

I slowly leaned off the cliff and fell like rain. The monster's eager tentacles reached towards me and dragged me deep into the murky sea. My face was filled with content; I did not weep for I was glad to go. I smiled because I would finally be given love. All that is good had perished from the universe forever, and so must I.

To be continued…